MERMAID PRECINCT

MERMAID PRECINCT

Keith R.A. DeCandido

eBooks
Pennsville, NJ

PUBLISHED BY
eSpec Books LLC
Danielle McPhail, Publisher
PO Box 242,
Pennsville, New Jersey 08070
www.especbooks.com

ISBN: 978-1-942990-92-5
ISBN (ebook): 978-1-942990-91-8

Interior Design: Danielle McPhail
Sidhe na Daire Multimedia
www.sidhenadaire.com

Cover Design: Mike McPhail
Current Design based on previous cover design by Jenn Reese
www.tigerbrightstudios.com

Art Credits - www.fotolia.com
Mermaid Medallion © Yakutsenya Marina
Sword © Cake78

Dedicated to all my
incredibly patient Kickstarter supporters.
You're the best.

ACKNOWLEDGMENTS

THANKS TO DANIELLE ACKLEY-MCPHAIL, MIKE MCPHAIL, AND GREG Schauer of eSpec Books, who rescued this series, republishing the previous books and agreeing to publish this and the next two novels, plus another short story collection. ("Two novels?" I hear you cry. "But we're out of precincts!" Yes, and no. All will be revealed in Chapter 1 of this book, trust me.)

My wife, Wrenn Simms, who helped me plot out this book during one of our long-drive kibbitz sessions that has resulted in some of my best fiction. GraceAnne Andreassi DeCandido, a.k.a. The Mom, who as ever served as a fine first reader, beating my drafts into shape. My agent, Lucienne Diver, who keeps the paperwork mills grinding as per usual.

Thanks to all the usual suspects: The Forebearance, Meredith Peruzzi, Matthew Holcombe, David Snowdeal, Lilly Hayes, Anneliese Hopwood, Sasquatch Nelson, and the late, very much lamented Dale Mazur, my dear brother-in-law and housemate, whom we still miss every damn day.

But the most thanks go to the following, who supported this book on Kickstarter: Danielle Ackley-McPhail, Benjamin Adler, Lorraine Anderson, Tom B., Emily Baisch, Linda Balder, Stephen Ballentine, balooster, Matthew Barr, Fred Bauer, Diane Bellomo, Todd Bennett, Michael Bentley, Jeremy Bottroff, Kiri Breese-Garelick, Jason Burns, Michael A. Burstein, Dennis P. Campbell, Rose Marie Caratozzolo, Marion F. Carpenter Jr., Danny Chamberlain, Chris, Caren Christiansen, Christopher, Anne Code, Brendan Coffey, Rachel Cooper, Corey, Amanda Cornwell, Mike Crate, Mary Catelynn Cunningham, Cyber Dave, Isaac "Will It Work" Dansicker, Alan Danziger, Todd Dashoff, Dwight Davis, Barbara deBary-Kesner, Annie Grainia

Donahue, Heather Eberhardt, Dr. DéAnna Ernst, eSpec Books, Zachary Faneuf, Richard Fine, Will "scifantasy" Frank, John French, Eric Gasior, Rich Gonzalez, Tina Good, Michael Gordon, Oliver Graf, Robert Greenberger, Joe Greene, Jaq Greenspon, Chris Gren, Anna Gridneva, Darrell Z. Grizzle, Carol Guess, Andreas Gustafsson, Carol Gyzander, Jonathan Haar, Kay Hafner, James Hallam, Julie Harris, Shael Hawman, Sherrill Hayes, Morgan Hazelwood, Joan Hoffman, Lonni Holland, Andrew Holman, Tanya Huff, Jonathan Hurley, Jeffrey Imparato, Elizabeth Inglee-Richards, Nicholas Irish, Maya J, Carol Jones, Andrew Kaplan, Laura Kaplan, Vaidah Katz, D Kelly, Amy Keyes, Kit Kindred, David "Handlebar" Kingsley, Todd Kogutt, Sonia Koval, Stephen Lesnik, Rita Lewis, Jeff Linder, Stephanie Lucas, Zan Lynx, Siannan MacDuff, Mara, Marc Margelli, Rebecca McClannahan, David Medinnus, MissMelysse, John J. Ordover, Maree Pavletich, Meredith Peruzzi, John Peters, Christon Pierce, Linda Pierce, Dirk Plug, Tom Powers, Jill Moss Racop, Rachael Raffensperger, Barry Rice, Rivka, Joe Rixman, Suzanne Rosin, Sasquatch, Kate Savage, scantrontb, Raymond Seavey, Jack Scheer, Abbe Schneider, Jeff Schultz, William Schulz, Emmanuel Seyman, Subrata Sircar, Claudia Slaney, Eric Slaney, Lauren Smith, Peggy Davis Smith, Jonathan Spore, Mark Squire, Louis Srygley, Linda Holmes Stewart, Cecilia Tan, Scott Thede, Andrew Timson, Ariel Vitali, Judith Waidlich, Wanderer, Josh Ward, Everett A. Warren, Dave Weiner, Clint Wilcox, Brian York, and Mike Zipser. I love you all to little tiny bits.

ONE

AN EARLY AUTUMN BREEZE TICKLED LIEUTENANT DANTHRES TRESYLLIONE'S blonde hair as she stood impatiently on Albin Way wishing Lord Doval would hurry up and finish his speech.

As he'd only just started talking, Danthres was less than optimistic that its end would come any time soon.

"Today happens to be the first anniversary of my ascension to the lordship of this great city-state," Doval was saying, standing in front of the entryway to the newest construction in Cliff's End. "When I inherited the post following the death of my father, the great Lord Albin, I didn't imagine the first year would be so very eventful."

Danthres snorted. Next to her, Lieutenant Torin ban Wyvald, her partner in the Cliff's End Castle Guard, glanced at her and smiled inside his thin red goatee. The breeze barely stirred his close-cropped red hair.

She whispered to him as Doval carried on, "Funny how he's completely ignoring Blayk now."

"Can you blame him?" Torin whispered back.

The reign of Doval's older brother Blayk had begun with Albin's death and ended with Blayk's arrest and condemnation when it was revealed that he'd been responsible for his father's death, as well as an attempt on the life of the king and queen. His reign had been barely a month long.

"No, but I can be annoyed, since we were the ones who found Blayk out and had him arrested."

Doval was still droning on. "...at midwinter, the incorporation of the prison barge into the Castle Guard as Manticore Precinct, and most recently the expansion of the docks. Then, of course, there was the fire in Barlin. I must say that I am very proud of how this great city-state responded to the sudden influx of refugees from our sister city, resulting in, among other things, this grand new section of town, named after my great father."

Again, Danthres snorted. Officially the neighborhood was called Albinton, but everyone had been calling it "New Barlin," since it was made up almost entirely of refugees from there. The origin of the fire that had devastated the city-state located to the west of here was still a mystery, as it had somehow managed to work past the fire-suppression spells provided by the Brotherhood of Wizards. However, that was a problem for Barlin's lord and lady and their people.

"The work done by the people of Cliff's End in clearing this section of the Forest of Nimvale and in constructing the buildings and thoroughfares of Albinton is a testament to why this is truly the finest city-state in all of Flingaria."

Danthres rolled her eyes. Looking around, she saw that all of her fellow lieutenants, as well as Captain Dru, looked just as uncomfortable as she felt.

Well, not quite all of her fellow lieutenants. Horran was conspicuously absent and would remain so—which made his lack of a replacement somewhat frustrating.

"Having said that," Doval continued, "our expansion has not been without its—ah, growing pains."

Dru let out a breath, but that was the closest anyone came to a groan. Danthres was grateful that at least nobody laughed at the awful joke.

"The riot during midsummer, the rampage of the so-called Gorvangin, and the general rise in crime since the establishment of Albinton, has forced us to expand the Castle Guard. Our recruitment drive has been quite the success, and today we officially open our newest branch: Phoenix Precinct!"

That prompted applause from the gathered crowd, which was mostly those selfsame new recruits, as well as a bunch of more experienced guards. Most of the latter were being assigned to this new precinct—they were all wearing the new phoenix crest on the chest of their leather armor. The new recruits had mostly been sent to Gryphon and Unicorn Precincts, which were the castle and the upper-class district, respectively. Those two precincts had the lightest duty—mostly it involved catering to the insane whims of the rich and tiresome—and Lord Doval, Sir Rommett (the member of the lord and lady's court in charge of appropriations and such for the Castle Guard), and Captain

Dru all agreed that it was best to put the new recruits there rather than in the new precinct. Phoenix was instead staffed by transfers from Dragon Precinct, the middle-class district; Goblin Precinct, the lower-class district; and Mermaid Precinct, the docklands.

A guard in a green cloak stepped toward the front as Doval waited for the applause to die down. Danthres tried not to snarl. "I still can't believe they promoted that shitbrain," she muttered.

Again, Torin smiled at her discomfort. "He *did* save young Dal Wint during midsummer."

"Which is the first useful thing he's done in fourteen years on the job."

"And now," Doval said, "may I present the officer in charge of the day shift at Phoenix Precinct, Sergeant Rik Slaney!"

Slaney waved to the crowd, with the same stupid smile he'd had on his face when he'd left Danthres to subdue a troll all by herself, back when they both served together in Goblin Precinct twelve years previous. He'd had a mostly uneventful career, working first in Goblin, then Dragon Precinct. It was serving there during midsummer that he saved the life of the son of the construction ministers, Sir and Madam Wint. Given all the new buildings and roads going up all around the demesne, the Wints had become two of the most influential and powerful members of the court. Slaney's promotion to sergeant was inevitable.

Doval went on: "He will be joined by Sergeant Ander Kaplan, who will be taking the night shift. He's home in bed right now, of course, resting up for his first shift this evening. Sergeant Slaney, please say a few words."

The smile fell from Slaney's face, and a look of abject fear spread across his features. That change was proportional to Danthres's own improvement in mood, as she went from annoyance at Slaney's promotion to total glee at how scared and helpless he suddenly looked at the thought of speaking in front of all these people.

"Well, uh, I mean—" Slaney swallowed. "I ain't much for, uh, for public speakin', really, but, uh—well, I guess I just wanna say 'at 's' an honor to, uh, t'be in charge'a this, well, this new, um, precinct, and I'm 'opin', um, this'll mean, y'know, that New Barlin'll be, um, safer and, ah, sounder, like, y'know?"

Doval visibly winced at Slaney's use of "New Barlin," which gave Danthres even more joy.

From the other side of her, Lieutenant Manfred whispered to her, "Roll call's gonna be a nightmare if that's how he talks to the troops."

Danthres chuckled. "And that's one of his more lucid speeches."

"Tell me about it—I had to work with him in Dragon, back in the day."

Captain Dru shot them both a look and put a finger to his lips.

"Er, well, thank you, Sergeant." Doval had obviously been expecting a longer speech. "Without further ado—guards of Phoenix Precinct, consider your first day shift to have officially begun!"

TWO

AFTER THE NEW GUARDS WENT INSIDE, LED BY SLANEY, CAPTAIN DRU HAD HIS people join Lord Doval to escort him back to the castle, along with several of the new recruits who were assigned to Gryphon Precinct. They proceeded around the periphery of New Barlin on Albin Way.

"My apologies," Doval said to Dru, "for making your detectives into a literal castle guard, but I'm afraid that it's not always safe to walk the streets of Cliff's End. I'm hoping this new precinct will change that."

"Me, too, m'lord," Dru said. Then he smiled. "Besides, we're all goin' to the same place."

"Indeed." Doval smiled back.

Dru hadn't been sure what to make of the new lord of the demesne a year ago when he took over from his brother, but Dru — who himself had been elevated to the captaincy at the same time — had found it to be a very productive working relationship. Doval was friendlier than your average rich twit, and didn't mind a little bit of familiarity from his subordinates. This was a huge relief, as being formal had never been one of Dru's strong suits. His discomfort with the strictures of the upper classes had been one of the reasons why he'd been hesitant to take the job initially.

The better pay was enough to overcome that hesitation, of course. As was getting off the streets. He'd already lost his partner, Hawk, killed during a bank robbery, and his heart was no longer in detective work after that. It was safer in the castle, a fact appreciated by both him and his wife.

Speaking of being safe... "Since we're on the subject of dangerous streets, m'lord, we're still down a detective."

"Yes, of course, Captain, my apologies. I'm afraid we've been so focused on increasing the guard ranks for Phoenix that replacing poor Lieutenant Horran has not been a financial priority."

"Maybe, m'lord, but it's becomin' a serious policin' priority. Honestly, we could use two more detectives on top of Horran's replacement."

"That will not be possible, I'm afraid, Captain, at least not yet," Doval said as they reached the easternmost part of the circular thoroughfare named for Lord Albin and proceeded on Boulder Pass. That would take them to Meerka Way, the main street, named for Doval's mother, the lady of the demesne and Albin's widow. Meerka Way ran from the castle all the way to the docks.

Dru was about to object when Doval continued, "However, you are correct that replacing Horran is long overdue. How is the lieutenant faring, by the way?"

"The healers've done everything they can," Dru said. "I just visited him last week, actually. He's in pretty good spirits for a guy whose legs were crushed by a crazy dwarf."

"Those Gorvangin thugs were quite disruptive," Doval said with a sigh.

"That's an understatement, m'lord." Horran wasn't the only guard who suffered a career-ending injury during the Gorvangin rampages.

"Nonetheless, you are correct that Horran must be replaced. Did you have a particular guard in mind to promote?"

"Actually, yeah. Remember the Phale case?"

Doval actually shuddered at that. "Quite well, Captain. Madam Phale was quite—insistent in her urgings for you to solve the case."

Dru hid a grin. He'd been grateful at the time that Madam Phale felt comfortable going over everyone's head straight to the lord of the demesne, rather than crawl up the asses of the lieutenants who had caught the case.

"Manfred and Kellan said they never would've closed it without the help of a guard from Unicorn named Dannee Ocly. She's a—"

Doval interrupted as they turned onto Meerka Way. "I'm actually familiar with Ocly. Her father was one of the finest dwarven architects extant, and I met him when I lived in Iaron. Her mother was an actor, and the first human to perform the lead in *Shansheria*. I saw her perform in Barlin."

"Yeah, Dannee lived in Barlin up until 'bout five years ago," Dru said.

"Indeed. I was thinking she might be a good person to have in Phoenix Precinct, to be honest. The people there might appreciate someone familiar with their former home."

"She'd be even better t'have in the east wing'a the castle, m'lord."

"Hm." Doval rubbed his chin, which after a year, Dru had come to recognize as what the noble did when he'd decided on a course of action, but wasn't sure he wanted to commit to it yet. Usually he came up with a feeble excuse in order to delay a final decision.

Sure enough, Doval asked, "Won't that be a bit odd, having two half-breeds in the squadroom? There's already Lieutenant Tresyllione, and now we'll have Ocly."

"I don't think it'll matter. Only person who might've had a problem's Aleta, and she's pretty much over that." It had been one of the nightmares of Dru's nascent captaincy, as Aleta lothLathna was an erstwhile member of the Shranlaseth. As one of the Elf Queen's former special forces (disbanded during the elven war for reasons that nobody had ever made clear), Aleta's disdain for mixed breeds was cranked up to its highest level. It had taken her a while to accept Danthres. Not that Danthres's attitude helped matters.

But after the lothHanthra murder, they'd started to come to a rapprochement. They still didn't like each other, but at least they were able to work together—which was necessary, since Aleta had had to be teamed up with various other detectives since Horran's injury.

"Oh, very well, as long as you don't think it'll be disruptive, Captain, I hereby approve it. I'll inform Sir Rommett."

"Thank you very much, m'lord. Can you excuse me, please?"

"Absolutely."

Peeling off due to sighting a member of the youth squad, one of the young people who ran errands for the Castle Guard, Dru tossed a copper at her and said, "Hey, Gerr! Get over to Unicorn Precinct and tell Sergeant Arron to send Dannee Ocly to the east wing of the castle."

Nodding, Gerr headed off after pocketing the copper.

Before Dru could rejoin Doval, a voice cried out, "*Cobarnag Gorvangin!*" At the same time, a rock flew through the air and almost hit Doval. It did strike one of the new recruits assigned to Gryphon, who fell to the ground like a sack of flour.

Three more guards, one of whom was Danthres, grabbed the rock thrower and pinned him to the street.

"Get him over to Dragon, have Sergeant Grint put his ass in the hole!" Dru cried out. "And someone get a healer for, uh—" He snapped his fingers.

Another guard, whose name Dru also couldn't remember, said, "Xarik, sir!"

"Right, Xarik. Get a healer for 'im."

Doval was watching as the two guards who weren't Danthres took the rock thrower away. Said perpetrator was crying, "*Cobarnag Gorvangin!*" over and over again.

"Will we never be rid of these fanatics?" Doval asked. "The entire leadership of Gorvangin has been put in the dungeons. Why are their followers still causing problems?"

Danthres brushed dirt off her brown cloak. "A copper'll get you a silver, my lord, that he's just a shitbrain who wants to cause trouble and throw rocks at people and is just using Gorvangin as an excuse."

"She's right," Dru said. "It's just some kids blowing off steam. But in case it ain't—" He turned to three of the guards from Gryphon. "You three, stay close to Lord Doval."

"Yes, sir," one of them said.

Dru really needed to learn the new guards' names.

The group proceeded to move forward up Meerka Way, crossing Oak Way into Unicorn Precinct. Dru hoped that the crazy would be more toned down here—or at least be less overt.

Aleta lothLathna walked up to move alongside the captain, Manfred and Arn Kellan behind her. "I couldn't help overhear part of your conversation with Lord Doval before that lunatic arrived. Am I to understand that I'm *finally* getting a new partner, Captain?" The elf's tone was respectful, an aspect of Aleta's personality that Dru had always appreciated.

"*Please* is she getting a new partner?" Manfred asked much more plaintively.

"Like, soon?" Kellan asked.

Nodding, Dru said, "We're promotin' Dannee Ocly from Unicorn."

"Ooh," Kellan said, "good choice. She's a smart one."

"I dunno," Manfred said, "she's kinda—I dunno, *nice.*"

Dru stared at the lieutenant. "What's wrong with nice?"

"In this job, it can get you killed."

With a cheeky grin, Dru said, "I wouldn't know. Look, Aleta can be mean enough for two people, so they'll be fine together."

Smirking, Aleta said, "Thank you, Captain."

Manfred frowned. "You sure it'll be okay? I mean, Dannee's half dwarf."

Chuckling, Kellan said, "Well, that means she only has to dislike half of her."

Aleta rolled her eyes. "Will both of you stop it, please? I'm fine with whomever Captain Dru pairs me with."

The cheeky grin still in place, Dru said, "That's because anything's trading up from her first partner after she made lieutenant."

That got Aleta to return the smile. "On the contrary, Captain, I doubt I'll ever top that first partner."

In truth, Aleta had carried Dru during their brief partnership before the latter's promotion, as he'd still been traumatized from Hawk's murder.

He just hoped that bringing Ocly on as a detective, along with the opening of a new precinct, would help keep things under control. His first few months as captain had been fantastic. Crime was at an all-time low in the wake of Lord Albin's death and Lord Blayk's disgrace.

And then there'd been the fire in Barlin. Since then, it had been utter chaos, and there was more than one occasion when Dru thought it was all going to come apart—especially when Horran went down.

Now, though, they had more guards, a new precinct, and he was back at a full complement of detectives. True, Sir Rommett had put a freeze on overtime requests after midsummer, but you couldn't have everything. Dru knew how useful OT was for the guards; he'd certainly appreciated it back when he was a guard and when he was a lieutenant. But maybe things would quiet down enough now that OT wouldn't be needed.

Danthres came over to join the group. "Did I hear correctly that lothLathna's finally getting a proper partner?"

"Yeah, you did," Dru said. "You should tell Torin."

Next to her, Torin frowned. "I'm right here, Dru."

"Oh, yeah, that is you. Sorry, didn't recognize you."

Torin scowled, having apparently wearied of the joke. "I'm not growing the full beard back nor letting my hair grow long again. Jak likes the way I look right now."

Giving Danthres a pleading look, Dru asked, "You're his partner, can't you get him to look the way he's supposed to?"

"I've been trying for a month now," Danthres said.

Hope in his heart, Dru asked, "But you haven't given up?"

Favoring her partner with a vicious grin, Danthres said, "Never."

"If you think you'll wear me down by constantly harping on my new look, I'm afraid you'll be disappointed, Danthres."

"We'll see."

Manfred shook his head. "True love. Helluva thing, huh?"

"I don't know if it is true love," Torin said quickly.

"C'mon, Torin," Kellan said with a laugh. "You cut your damn hair for this carpenter. I'm surprised the back of your neck and your cheeks didn't burst in to flames from their first-ever exposure to sunlight."

"If that ain't true love," Manfred added, "I dunno what is."

Dru shook his head and chuckled. It still freaked him out seeing Torin with short hair and a goatee, but Dru supposed he would have to live with it as long as Torin was involved with Jak Reesh. Maybe they'd break up and things would get back to normal.

He realized that was a horrible thing to think, but he couldn't help it. Torin looked *really bizarre* with short hair...

THREE

GONZAL WALKED SLOWLY DOWN THE DOCKS, JAYSON BY HIS SIDE. SINCE midsummer, Sergeant Mannit had insisted that all guards work in pairs in Mermaid Precinct. It was for everyone's safety. As it was, there were dozens of sailors eyefucking the pair of them, just waiting for an opening to pounce.

At least, that was how Gonzal saw it. He'd stopped saying it, though, because Jayson kept giving him shit about it.

"Ah, that breeze feels nice."

Gonzal looked at Jayson as if he were insane. "What breeze?"

"Can't you feel the breeze?"

Shrugging, Gonzal said, "Yeah, I guess there's a little breeze, but so what? We're right on the Garamin Sea, there's *always* a breeze."

"So you should be able to feel it," Jayson said slowly.

"Whatever, look, I'm more worried about those guys over there." Gonzal pointed at the group of sailors who were staring at them.

"'Ey! Swords!" one of them said, pulling away from the crowd.

Gonzal recognized him as Abo, the first mate of the *Breeze*. He also recalled that the *Breeze* had been impounded by the Brotherhood of Wizards a week ago, which explained why Abo was just loitering on the docks.

Holding up both hands, Gonzal said, "We don't want no trouble, Abo."

"Easy, Gonzie, just askin' a couple questions, is all. Jus' wonderin' if you know when they're gonna take the *Breeze* outta hock."

"Oh, for Temisa's sake, Abo, it's the *brotherhood*."

Jayson added, "I'd put a copper down on a few years after never, m'self."

"Dammit."

"So instead'a waitin' 'round for your boat to come back," Jayson said, "you should be finding yourself a new one to sign on to."

"As what, a deckhand?" Abo drew himself up to his full height. "I'm a first mate, and a damn good one to boot!"

"But all the boats have first mates?" Gonzal said.

Abo deflated, slouching again. "Yeah. Shit, I'm s'posed to be captain! Whole reason I let you lot know about the contraband scrolls was so I could get to be captain! Didn't think they'd be takin' the damn *boat*."

"Things are tough all over." Gonzal shrugged. "Look, I can ask Sergeant Mannit, all right?"

"Thanks, Gonzie."

Gonzal didn't add that the sergeant's response would be gales of laughter. The brotherhood never gave back things they impounded.

"'Ey," Abo said before the two guards could continue on their way. "I heard tell that Horran got himself messed up by those Gorvangin shitbrains. He okay?"

"You knew Horran?"

Abo's squinty eyes went wide. "'Knew'? He ain't dead, is he?"

Quickly, Jayson said, "No, he ain't." He glared at Gonzal. "For Wiate's sake, don't scare people like that."

"Yeah, Gonzie," Abo said, "had me worried, there."

"No, sorry," Gonzal said, "he's fine. Well, no, he ain't fine, but he's alive. Legs got crushed."

"I'm gonna see 'im tomorrow night," Jayson said. "Me and some'a the boys are headin' up to visit him."

Gonzal frowned. "You are?"

"Yeah. Weren't you invited? Lavian put it together."

The frown turned into a scowl. "That shitbrain owes me a silver. No wonder he didn't invite me."

Abo shook his head. "Well, you tell old Horran that Abo sends his best. We miss his ugly face down here."

"We all did after he got promoted last year," Gonzal said.

"I will. Thanks, Abo," Jayson put in. "And good luck!"

Scowling, Abo said, "Yeah, I'm gonna need it."

The pair of them continued to walk toward the end of the dock and the new extension being constructed. The crowds thinned out, which meant there would be less here for them to do, but at least it was a moment to get away from the bigger crowds.

"Think Abo'll be all right?" Jayson asked.

"I dunno." Gonzal sighed. "He's right, he should have his own boat by now. Sucks to go from first mate to nothin', all 'cause he did the right thing turnin' his captain in."

Jayson snorted. "You're joking, right?"

Gonzal stared at his fellow guard. "No, why?"

"You think Captain Hlorahk was the only one involved with that smugglin'? Whole ship was in on it. Abo just wanted to be captain, is all. Thought turnin' the captain in was his ticket."

"Shitty way to treat your captain, you ask me."

"Damn right." Jayson started walking back toward the center of the dock, then stopped.

Gonzal noticed that two more dockrats were staring openly at them. These guys looked a lot meaner than Abo.

Jayson, though, then turned around. "Uh, Gonz, they ain't starin' at us."

Turning, Gonzal saw that a dinghy was moving slowly toward the dock. That, in and of itself, wasn't unusual, but it was flying a black flag.

"Shit. Pirates." Gonzal turned and headed toward the part of the dock the dinghy was moving toward.

"Um." Jayson didn't move alongside him.

Stopping and turning to face his comrade, Gonzal asked, "What?"

"That ain't just any pirate. Lookit the flag."

Turning back toward the Garamin, Gonzal peered more closely at the flag, which had the traditional skull and crossbones of a pirate flag.

But then he squinted and saw that the skull had a crown of lilies slightly askew on its head. And the two bones were also bound together by a vine of lilies.

"Temisa drown me now," Gonzal muttered. "It's the Pirate Queen."

"Wiate's teeth." Jayson shook his head. "I don't think she's ever come to Cliff's End."

"Me either." Gonzal just stared at the dinghy. Only one person was in it, a male human.

"I wonder what she wants," Jayson said.

Gonzal shrugged. "Dunno, but it can't be much. I mean, I heard she was eight feet tall and breathed fire."

Jayson turned to stare at Gonzal. "Breathes fire? You know that boats are made outta wood, right?"

"Yeah, I guess."

45

"Then what good's breathing fire gonna do her except to burn up her boats?"

Again, Gonzal shrugged. "They're on the water, easy enough to put the fire out, right?"

Rolling his eyes, Jayson turned to look back at the dinghy. "I heard she ran the elven blockade back during the war."

"Way I heard it," Gonzal said, "she paid bribes to the Elf Queen to be let through the blockade."

Jayson stared at Gonzal. "She *helped* the Elf Bitch?"

Gonzal shrugged a third time. "She's a damn pirate, whaddaya expect?"

As the dinghy reached the dock, Gonzal gestured to catch the rope that would secure the dinghy to the dock. The pirate tossed the rope, which Gonzal caught unerringly and immediately wrapped around the post.

While he did that, Jayson asked, "What brings the Pirate Queen to Cliff's End?"

Rather than answer directly, the pirate asked a question of his own. "Is there still a halfbreed woman in the Castle Guard detective squad?"

"Hate the detectives," Gonzal muttered as he checked to make sure the pirate's rope was secure. "They think they're all smarter'n us."

"That's because they *are* smarter'n us." Jayson shook his head. "I'm assumin' you mean Lieutenant Tresyllione?"

The pirate nodded. "Yes, her. Is she still with the Castle Guard?"

Gonzal grinned. "'Less she died'a alcohol poisoning from drinkin' at the Chain last night, yeah she is." By the time Gonzal had finished his post-shift drinking at the Old Ball and Chain last night, Danthres Tresyllione was on her fourth ale while her partner, Torin ban Wyvald, was walking to the bar to fetch her fifth.

"Could you summon her, please?"

"The hell's the Pirate Queen need with a detective?"

The pirate had been real quiet-like, and looking down at the deck of the dinghy the whole time, but now he looked up. Gonzal saw that he looked pretty upset. "The Cap'n, sadly, has no need for anything ever again. She's dead, and we believe she's been murdered—and we'd like the Castle Guard to investigate her death."

FOUR

TORIN BAN WYVALD LOOKED ON HIS PARTNER WITH CONCERN AS THEY worked their way down Meerka Way toward the docks. By the time they crossed Axe Way into Goblin Precinct—and the street got far more crowded—Torin moved alongside her and asked, "Are you all right?"

"I'm honestly not. I can't believe she's dead."

Torin blinked. Danthres always felt strongly about people being killed, but it was generally in the abstract. The tone in her voice now, though, was different, as if she'd lost a friend. "You know—or knew, rather—the Pirate Queen?"

Danthres nodded. "She used to come to Sorlin fairly regularly. Her flagship, the *Rising Jewel*, was one of the few boats that could get close to Sorlin's coastline without being damaged. And she used to bring halfbreeds to us for sanctuary." Danthres had spent her formative years in Sorlin, a haven for people who violated elven purity laws by interbreeding with other races. They later kicked her out for being a disruptive influence following the accidental death of her best friend. A year ago the community itself disbanded, since elven purity laws had been a thing of the past since the Elf Queen's death at the end of the war a dozen years previous. The community had gone below subsistence levels. Danthres's feelings on that particular subject had run the gamut over the past year, ranging from disinterest to anger to sadness.

"I'm surprised," Torin said. "I didn't realize that pirates engaged in altruism."

"Of course they do—well, she did, anyhow. I have to admit, her crew are the only pirates I'm personally familiar with. And I've heard nothing from them since moving here to Cliff's End."

"Nor I," Torin said, "beyond the stories one hears from bards and such. Hardly surprising. Pirates work best in solitude, and when they do dock somewhere, it out of necessity would be a place that receives considerably less boat traffic than we receive in Cliff's End." He smiled. "It would also be a place that doesn't have a huge law-enforcement agency like the Castle Guard."

"True." Danthres sighed. "She went through the blockade several times to rescue children—not just halfbreeds, but also full-blooded children who were left orphaned by the war."

That surprised Torin. "I didn't realize you took in full-bloods."

"We took in *anybody*. That was the point. Yes, most of our population were halfbreed elves, because they were hunted down everywhere else, but we took in plenty of others."

By this time, they'd reached the River Walk, bringing them to Mermaid Precinct. It was midday, and several of the fishing ships had come in or were coming in with the day's catch, which would be many people's dinners tonight.

Snaking their way through the crowds—the increase in Cliff's End's population made the docks a nightmare to navigate, especially around midday—all conversation ceased, as the crowds and noise made it impossible to speak audibly. By the time they made it to the far end of the precinct, where the new dock extension was being built, Torin felt physically exhausted from pushing his way through the crowds. Whatever inkling the populace might have had to step aside for members of the Castle Guard was no match for their desire to purchase fish at midday, it seemed.

Jayson and Gonzal from Mermaid Precinct were standing near a black dinghy. Torin noticed that it had a flagpole but no flag.

Gonzal stepped forward to greet the detectives. "Lieutenants. That's the Pirate Queen's sailing master. S'all he'd say, though, 'cept that the Pirate Queen's dead, and he wants you two—well, you, Lieutenant Tresyllione—t'be the ones t'investigate."

Danthres barely acknowledged Gonzal before continuing forward.

Indicating the dinghy with his head, Torin asked, "Is the boat not flying a flag?"

"Oh, it was, but we asked the gentleman t'take it down. Figured it'd attract attention, y'know?"

"Good idea," Torin said.

He then jogged to catch up with Danthres, who was approaching the dinghy. "Lisson? Is that you?"

The gentleman on the boat broke into a huge grin. "It *is* you! The Cap'n said you were workin' for the Castle Guard doin' detective work—heard you solved Gan Brightblade's murder."

"We both did," Torin said. "I'm her partner, Lieutenant Torin ban Wyvald."

Lisson frowned. "Ban Wyvald? You're the Chief Artisan of Myverin's son?"

"No longer—now I'm the High Magistrate's son, as my father was promoted."

"You'll be amused to know that there was a bounty for you during the war. Cap'n thought about trying to track you down—least that's what I heard. I was just a deckhand back then."

"Which is when I knew him," Danthres said. "So the Captain is dead?"

Nodding, Lisson said, "Yes, and we believe she was murdered. I'd like you to come with us to *Rising Jewel* and investigate."

"Why won't you bring your ship here?" Torin asked.

"I doubt we could fit all three of her boats here," Danthres said with a glance at her partner.

"Actually," Lisson said with a sigh, "it's just the one ship. The Cap'n got rid of *Heart of Silver* and *Dwyte's Revenge*."

"How come?" Danthres sounded surprised.

"It became too difficult to wrangle three ships. And our numbers have been down consistently over the past few years—too many crew retiring, not enough replacements. In any case, if you step onto the dinghy with me, I can take you to—"

Torin folded his arms over the gryphon medallion etched into the chest of his leather armor. "Absolutely not."

Lisson frowned. "Whyever not?"

"You expect us to simply hand ourselves over as your prisoners?"

"You won't be our prisoners. We wish you to investigate the Cap'n's death, as I said."

"And why should we believe that you'd do this?"

Lisson smirked. "Well, your Castle Guard does have a reputation for solving such murders. Even of famous figures in Flingaria—not just Gan Brightblade and Olthar lothSirhans, but also I believe you uncovered Lord Blayk's conspiracy to murder his father Lord Albin."

Torin waved an arm back and forth. "It's nothing to do with that. You're *pirates*. It's difficult to trust you under the best of circumstances. You mentioned my father — a year ago, he attempted to bring me home. Obviously, he did not succeed. Just enough time has passed for him to have returned to Myverin in failure and for the council to then put out a bounty on my head to make another attempt. For that matter, Danthres and I have made many enemies outside Cliff's End — two years ago, we exposed a wealthy gentleman in Treemark who was hoarding Hamnau gems. The Brotherhood of Wizards confiscated them. For that matter, I can't imagine that the conspiracy Lord Blayk masterminded only involved him. And those are just the people I can think of off the top of my head who might wish to pay for us to be captured and brought to them. I'm afraid that sailing with you to your boat is out of the question."

For a moment, Torin feared that Danthres would go against his feeling, letting her familiarity with the Pirate Queen cloud her judgment.

Luckily, his partner was smarter than that, which was one of the reasons why he liked being her partner.

"Torin's right," she said. "We'll need more if we're to go with you."

"You *knew* the Cap'n, Danthres, don't you wish to give her justice?"

"Yes, I *knew* her — two decades ago. All I know of her since is her reputation, which, as my partner has cogently pointed out, is as a pirate. By definition, her life — and yours — is one of criminality, and our function is to stop criminals, not help them. And we have nothing to prove what you say."

Lisson stared at her for a second, looking disappointed. Torin would gladly live with that disappointment, and was prepared to turn around and wade through the crowds at the docks to go back to the castle.

However, Lisson then put his hand over his heart and said, "I swear by the soul of Dwyte that I speak the truth when I say that the Cap'n is dead, and we wish you to investigate her death as you would any murder in Cliff's End. I also swear by the soul of Dwyte that you will come to no harm on *Rising Jewel* and will be returned to the dock when your work is done."

Before Torin could scoff at that, Danthres said, "Very well. Let's go."

"Excuse me?" Torin couldn't believe what he was hearing. "One oath and you trust this — this *criminal*?"

"Yes," Danthres said, "because the oath is sworn on the soul of the greatest pirate who ever lived. Dwyte was the pirate who harried Baron Alomgord's forces for years. Any pirate who goes back on that oath is put to death."

Lisson regarded Torin intently. "I have never before sworn that oath, Lieutenant ban Wyvald—because nobody has ever doubted my word in the past. Yes, I am a pirate, but that simply means I live beyond the laws of mortal governments—as do we all. We do, however, live by our own code, and the most sacrosanct part of that code is to swear on Dwyte's soul."

Danthres put a hand on his shoulder. "Torin, trust me. Please."

Torin sighed. "Very well. *You*, I trust, Danthres, always. If you believe this oath will protect us, then I will agree to sail to the pirate ship."

"Thank you." Lisson's words were passionate, and heartfelt, and Torin almost believed in their sincerity.

"We should also send for Boneen," Torin added.

"Who is that?" Lisson asked.

"Our magickal examiner," Danthres said. "A mage on loan from the Brotherhood of Wizards. He casts a spell that enables him to see what happened in a particular place in the past."

Lisson shook his head. "That would be a waste of time, I'm afraid. *Rising Jewel* is quite heavily warded against all spells."

Torin's eyes widened. "*All* spells?"

"It was a *very* expensive undertaking—and quite all encompassing. I think that's also truly part of why she pared down to a single ship. Renewing the wards is even more costly."

"Very well, though that will make the process more complicated," Torin said with a sigh.

Danthres shrugged as she stepped onto the dinghy. "It's not as if it's the first time we've been unable to work with a peel-back."

"True." Torin turned to Gonzal and Jayson. "Send a message to Captain Dru, please, and let him know where we're going and what we're doing." He hesitated, then added, "If we're not back by the end of shift, assume that we've been kidnapped by the Pirate Queen."

"Torin!" Danthres said.

"Forgive me, Danthres, but I prefer to have a contingency in case your old friend here whom you haven't seen in two decades is an unscrupulous pirate who goes back on his word."

Lisson gazed at Danthres. "Your friend is quite obdurate."

"My *partner* is correct in his misgivings. He doesn't know you and has no reason to trust you. For that matter, as he points out, I haven't seen you in some time. Do you blame us for taking steps to ensure our safety?"

"I suppose not." He lowered his head and sighed. "Forgive me, Danthres, but the Cap'n's death—"

She put a hand on his shoulder. "I understand." Then she looked up at Torin. "Shall we?"

Nodding, Torin also hopped onto the dinghy. "Let us go to our aquatic crime scene."

FIVE

MANFRED WAS TRYING VERY HARD NOT TO GIGGLE WATCHING ALETHA lothLathna "training" her new partner, the freshly promoted Lieutenant Dannee Ocly.

"So when you're done with the report—" Aleta started, pointing at a scroll that contained the report on the Gorf case that she'd been forced to close on her own, since the other four detectives had been busy with other cases.

Dannee didn't let her finish, of course. "I sign it and then give it to Ep. We can summon him through that window." She pointed a stubby finger at the picture window that showed the amazing view of the Forest of Nimvale. After a year, Manfred was still captivated by the beauty of the forest as seen through that window, especially watching it change with the seasons. (It was amazing at midwinter.)

Aleta let out a long sigh. "Would it be too much to ask that I be permitted to finish a sentence once in a while?"

"Oh, I'm so sorry!" Dannee's face fell. Her visage had the compressed quality usually seen in dwarves, complete with the mustache common to dwarven women, and it looked hilarious all wide and frightened like that. Not to mention that face, the coarse hair of a dwarf, and the small hands and stubby fingers of a dwarf all on someone who was the same height as Manfred himself. "It's just—I've been waiting for this day for *so long*, and—" She shook her head. "I'm sorry, Lieutenant. Please, continue."

Now Aleta smiled indulgently. "It's all right. And you should call me Aleta. We're colleagues now."

"Right, right, right, I keep forgetting."

"I was the same way," Manfred said from his desk. "Torin kept having to remind me to call him, uh, Torin."

Kellan came into the squadroom with Sergeant Jonas.

"Hey, partner," Manfred said. "All done with the magistrate?"

Nodding, Kellan hung his cloak up on the pegboard before moving to sit at his desk, which was next to Manfred's. "Yeah. Gave him five years."

Slamming his hand on the desk, making the scrolls on it bounce and startling the others in the squadroom, Manfred stood up angrily. "Dammit, that's the minimum sentence."

Dannee made an "eeep!" noise and cringed, while Aleta immediately went for her sword before realizing it was just Manfred letting off steam.

"What is it *now*?" Aleta asked, taking her gloved hand off the hilt of her sword.

"Avnarro got the minimum for robbing those stands down Jorbin's Way."

Dannee rubbed her furry chin. "Five years is still a *really* long time when you're all alone on the barge. Don't you think he'll be miserable enough?"

Kellan stared up at him. "C'mon, it was his first offense, we caught him in about ten seconds, and he confessed before we could even ask him anything. He knows it was stupid, and he'll spend five years on the barge realizing he was stupid, and we'll never see him again because he'll be scared shitless. This guy wasn't your criminal mastermind, y'know?" He grinned. "'Sides, that isn't the important part."

Manfred frowned. In truth, Dannee's comment had extinguished his frustration, and he sat back down. "What's the important part?"

"We've now closed twelve cases in a row, all of which resulted in imprisonment or execution. That's *gotta* be a record."

"Not hardly," Jonas said. "Nael and Karistan hit thirteen in a row twice, and so did Iaian and Linder once."

"Fine," Manfred said, "so we close our next case and—"

"And you'll be tied for third." Jonas smiled viciously. "The captain and Hawk hit fourteen in a row."

"So what's the record?" Kellan asked.

Aleta rolled her eyes. "Let me guess—Torin and Danthres?"

Jonas shook his head. "No, the most they've closed in a row has been six. No, the record is fifteen by two of the first people Captain Brisban hired to be detectives when Lord Albin first made the Castle Guard into an investigatory agency, Lieutenants Morlland and Jhimi."

"Fine." Manfred leaned back in his chair. "We just have to close three more cases, and we dethrone those two."

Kellan put his head in his hands. "Great, now you've jinxed it."

"Oh, stop it. There's no such thing."

"In my experience, Wiate doesn't waste much time yanking the rug out from under people who get too arrogant."

Manfred stuck his tongue out at his partner. "I'm not arrogant, we're just that good."

"You're lucky," Jonas said. "I was just a guard when Nael and Karistan had their streaks, but I can tell you this—they *weren't* great detectives. I mean, they were fine, don't get me wrong, but not great detectives. But they got lucky. And so did you."

"Hey, that's not fair," Kellan said. "Closing the Cuir Mak case took a lot of effort."

Jonas nodded. "And the next five cases after that were all so easy that one of the dumber guards could have closed them. The point is, these streaks aren't about skill, they're about luck *and* skill. Morlland and Jhimi barely even knew how to be detectives because the job was so new, but they managed to stumble their way into some easy cases— partly because some of the laws have changed since the Castle Guard was repurposed. Torin and Danthres have never closed more than half a dozen in a row, and they're better detectives than you'll ever be."

Aleta frowned. "That's not fair."

Jonas pointed at Manfred and Kellan. "Sorry, I was referring specifically to those two."

"Hey!" Kellan said. "*That's* not fair!"

"Who said life is fair? It's true. Eventually, you're gonna get a case you can't close. Happens to everyone. Might even be the next one through the door, since you two are up next."

The sergeant then went back out the door into the main part of the castle with his scrolls, his green cape billowing behind him.

"You realize he's full of shit, right?" Manfred said to Kellan.

"No, *you're* full of shit. Look, I admit, we've done some good work, but we've also had some easy ones."

As Kellan spoke, Aleta was saying to Dannee, "So now we file them with Ep. The thing about Ep is that he loses everything, and whatever he doesn't lose, he misfiles. I remember one time, Horran and I were trying to dig up an old file on a child abduction case from about five or six years back. Took three days for Ep to locate it."

"Really?" Dannee shook her head. "You know, I'd heard that about the imp, but I was surprised. In my experience, imps are very well organized."

Manfred's eyes went wide. "Excuse me?"

Kellan added, "Yeah, Dannee, your experience is *way* different from ours."

Dannee turned and regarded them curiously. "How many imps have you dealt with?"

"Um..." Kellan shifted in his chair. "Well, just this one..."

Manfred, though, had more of a leg to stand on than his partner. "Back when I first came up, I was assigned to Unicorn, and there was a domestic involving an imp. It was a big mess, the imp screwed *everything* up so bad. Ep's not as bad as that shitbrain imp was, but he's still pretty awful."

"That's *really* bizarre." Dannee looked at Aleta. "May I file the paperwork, please, Aleta?"

Holding up her hands, Aleta said, "I also need the file for the Abinori case. I'm testifying before the magistrate tomorrow on that one, and I want to go over it in the morning."

"I can do that, but why not wait until morning?"

Chuckling, Aleta said, "Haven't you been listening? It could take him that long to locate the file."

"It won't. I promise."

"All right." Aleta sounded as dubious as Manfred felt. "But if you lose your temper in frustration, we'll all understand."

With a pleasant smile, Dannee took the paperwork from the Gorf case and then approached the picture window.

She turned to Aleta. "I say the name of the case, right?"

Aleta nodded.

"*Sen fin heriox* Gorf."

Manfred blinked. "*What* did she just say?"

Kellan seemed stunned, and didn't answer—though the question was rhetorical in any case.

That didn't stop Aleta from answering. "I don't recognize any of those words. Well, except Gorf, obviously."

Even as they expressed their confusion, a portion of the window twisted and reformed into the bearded face of the imp.

Ep spoke in a similar tongue, though he spoke so fast, Manfred couldn't even make out the words.

"*Guvni fan hel heriox* Abinori," Dannee said as she placed the Gorf scroll into Ep's beard.

Another scroll came out a second later, which was the fastest Ep had ever retrieved a case file, wrong or right, in the year Manfred had been a lieutenant.

Some more rapid-fire gibberish from the imp, then both Ep and Dannee laughed heartily, and Dannee said, "*Ava say fon ava torc.*"

"Seefa." With that, the imp disappeared, turning back into a window.

"What—" Aleta shook her head and pointed at the window. "What *was* that?"

Dannee stared at the other three in amazement. "Don't any of you speak Imprata?"

Manfred slowly shook his head. "I have enough trouble with Common."

"I assume," Kellan asked, "that that's the imp's language?"

"I didn't even know they *had* a language," Manfred said.

"*Everyone* has a language," Aleta said witheringly. "But there was never any need to learn Imprata in the Shranlaseth."

"Startin' to think there's a need to learn it now," Manfred muttered.

"I can't believe you've never spoken to Ep in his own language!"

To Manfred's surprise, and relief, Dannee did not speak those words in a rebuking tone. She seemed genuinely surprised, but not upset.

That was okay, though, because he felt upset enough for them both.

Jonas came back in. "Manfred, Kellan, you've got your shot at number thirteen. Messenger just came from Sergeant Mannit. That Emmegan-paint graffiti has turned up again, and this time he wants a proper investigation."

"What's the big deal?" Manfred asked. "It's just some random shitbrain painting words on boats with magickally enhanced paint. Nobody's seen them, but it's Mermaid. Who cares?"

"A lot of people when it's Sir Louff's yacht."

Manfred winced.

"Fine," Kellan said, going to fetch his and Manfred's cloaks both. "Let's go see who vandalized a noble's yacht."

SIX

THE FIRST TIME DANTHRES TRESYLLIONE HAD SEEN THE *RISING JEWEL*, SHE'D been a child in Sorlin. She'd been standing on the cliffs that overlooked the Garamin Sea with her adoptive sister Lil, and the pair of them had watched in awe as this big beautiful boat, topped by a foreboding black flag, appeared out of the fog and slowly settled in among the reefs.

"What is that?" she'd asked, eyes wide with disbelief.

"It's a boat," Lil had replied with a twinkle in her eye.

"Very funny. I know it's a boat. What's it doing there?"

"Crashing and sinking, if it's like every other boat that's tried to approach from the Garamin." Part of why Sorlin had been founded on the Kone Peninsula was due to its coastline being a cliff above rocky reefs that were death on small boats and very damaging to large ones.

However, the *Rising Jewel* hadn't crashed or sunk, to Lil's surprise.

Rowing toward it now on the dinghy, approaching it directly from the sea, it loomed larger in Danthres's vision than it had from atop the peninsula cliffs back then.

As the dinghy approached, Danthres suddenly felt a tingle all up and down her body.

Torin shivered, so he obviously felt it as well. "What was *that*?"

Lisson smiled. "I told you the ship is quite heavily warded."

Gazing at Danthres, Torin said, "If the wards are so intense that *we're* feeling them, I shudder to think how Boneen would respond."

"Poorly." Danthres was, if anything, understating it. Boneen was cranky under the best of circumstances, and being confronted with wards of sufficient power that non-mages could feel them would be the worst of circumstances for him.

Someone on the deck threw a rope ladder over the side, and it bounced off the hull with a thunk.

Lisson pointed at the ladder. "After you, Lieutenants."

Torin shook his head. "After *you*, I would say."

Danthres sighed. On the one hand, yes, this *was* a pirate ship, but Torin was taking his mistrust to an absurd extreme.

He continued: "I suspect that your shipmates will be far more comfortable having the first face onto the deck being a familiar one rather than two armed and armored members of the local law-enforcement."

At that, Danthres relented. "My partner is correct."

Shrugging, Lisson said, "As you wish. I was merely attempting politeness."

"Hence our confusion." Torin grinned, a sight that still disconcerted Danthres without a huge red beard surrounding it. "We encounter very little of such in our line of work."

Lisson chuckled. "Nor do we."

The sailing master climbed up the ladder, and Danthres followed him up, Torin trailing behind her.

As she climbed up onto the deck, Danthres heard a deep voice say, "I still think this is a stupid idea."

Lisson replied, "We've already had this argument, Chamblin. And we agreed. They're here now, so let's let them do what they do best."

Settling onto the deck, Danthres turned and reached a hand out to Torin, guiding him onto the deck. They both turned as one to face a semicircle of pirates. Danthres recognized a couple of faces, but most were strangers—it *had* been almost two decades, so it was more of a surprise that she knew any of them beyond Lisson. Though the deck was bucking and bouncing with the tide while the ship was anchored, they all stood steadily.

Danthres couldn't really say the same. She struggled to keep her footing, and she could see that Torin was having similar difficulties.

At the center of the semicircle—which was effectively blocking the two detectives from actually going anywhere else on the vessel—was a gnome with dark hair and a deep scowl.

Pointing at the pair of them, Lisson said to the gnome, "These are the detectives: Lieutenant Danthres Tresyllione and her partner, Torin ban Wyvald. Lieutenants, this is Chamblin, the quartermaster."

Danthres recalled that the quartermaster was the equivalent of the ship's first mate—the second-in-command after the Pirate Queen herself. When she was a girl, it was an old man whose name she couldn't recall now two decades on.

Chamblin scoffed. "They're thugs in armor."

"They're more than that," Lisson said. "Danthres used to live in Sorlin, and I knew her then—so did the Cap'n. And Lieutenant ban Wyvald is from Myverin."

"Myverin's full'a shit-suckers."

Torin stepped forward, then stumbled. Danthres grabbed his arm to keep him from falling to the deck. "Thank you," he said to her, then looked back at Chamblin. "I agree with that assessment, which is indeed why I left."

Several of the pirates chuckled, though Chamblin, Danthres noted, wasn't one of them. She wasn't sure if they were making light of their unsteadiness afoot or Torin's rejoinder.

"The point," Lisson said, "is that he was raised there and attended the collegium. I can vouch for Danthres, and ban Wyvald's pedigree speaks for itself."

"And what will they tell us? That the Captain's dead? We already know that."

"They'll tell us who did it, so he may be punished."

"I doubt that."

"In case your doubts prove fruitless," Danthres said, "we should see the body."

For a moment, Danthres feared that Chamblin would not allow the semicircle to be broken and they'd be told to climb back down the ladder. Worse, Chamblin might do as Torin had feared and take them prisoner. He obviously didn't want them there, and his wishes would override those of Lisson, in theory, since he was now in charge.

Torin then moved back toward the rope ladder, falling more than stepping to the railing and grabbing it for purchase. "Come, Danthres, it's obvious that our services are not required here."

"Where do you think you're goin, shit-sucker?" the gnome asked.

"Back to Cliff's End. I shouldn't be surprised that you don't wish our aid. After all, we serve the cause of justice, and I see very little of that in the lives that you've chosen to lead."

A susurrus of anger flew through the assembled pirates, and Chamblin's scowl deepened, an action Danthres wouldn't have considered possible a moment earlier.

One of the crew asked, "You think we don't want justice for the Captain?"

"I think some of you do. Enough to have overridden the wishes of this gnome, who obviously doesn't want us here. But that discussion has already been had, or Lisson would never have come to fetch us in the first place. So I can only conclude that something has changed, and we are no longer needed or wanted. Therefore—"

"Stop." Chamblin stepped forward. "You really *are* from Myverin. You talk just like those shit-suckers." He turned, nodded to the assembled pirates, and they all stepped away, returning to their duties. "I agreed to let you try to find her killer, and I will abide by that agreement. But I have no intention of liking it." That last was said with a sneer at the sailing master. Lisson, for his part, was completely unabashed, which Danthres appreciated.

Pointedly looking away from Chamblin, Lisson said, "Let's go. She's in her cabin."

The two pirates led the way across the deck to a staircase below. Torin and Danthres followed behind, holding onto whatever they could to keep from falling gracelessly to the deck.

As they walked, Chamblin said, "We first realized something was wrong when the Captain didn't report for first watch."

"Cap'n *always* reports for first watch and is *never* late." Lisson sighed. "Or, was never late, anyhow."

The staircase and the corridor it emptied onto were barely narrow enough to accommodate the diminutive form of the quartermaster. Danthres found she had to walk sideways in order to fit, and Torin did likewise. The cramped corridor, at the very least, made it less likely that they would fall down with the bouncing deck.

"Came down here to her cabin to see what was wrong. I knocked, she didn't answer, and then I opened the door."

"She didn't lock it?" Torin asked.

Lisson shook his head. "She never did. Said her door was always open."

"She also said," Chamblin added, "that the whole boat was her quarters, this space was just where she slept."

The gnome opened the door to reveal a surprisingly sparse cabin. The bed had sheets made of Cormese silk, as well as a cotton blanket, but there was nothing else particularly lavish about the space.

The Pirate Queen herself lay on the bed, staring upward with dead black eyes.

"She barely seems to have aged a day."

Torin moved past Lisson and Chamblin to inspect the body on the bed. "This is what she looked like twenty years ago?" he asked.

Danthres nodded. "There are a few more lines on her face, but not much. Same raven hair, same dark eyes, same leathery skin."

"I'm assuming the blue tinge around her mouth is new."

Lisson nodded. "Rat poison."

"Of which we have a dozen barrels that the entire crew has access to," Chamblin said, "so don't even ask about that."

Danthres nodded. Rats were a universal constant in sea travel, and rat poison was a brutal necessity on a seafaring vessel if you didn't want your ship to get overrun. "When would she have been poisoned?"

"Hard to say." Lisson rubbed his bearded chin. "She eats with the crew, and we all dined together. But those dishes and mugs have long since been cleaned."

Torin looked around the cabin. "There appear to be no mugs or plates in here, either."

"Damn." Chamblin frowned. "She always kept a mug nearby. Sometimes it was ale, sometimes it was fruit juice, sometimes it was just water, but she always had a drink to hand."

"All in the same mug?" Danthres asked.

Lisson shook his head. "No, she always used a different one when she changed drinks. But she just grabbed whatever mug was clean in the galley."

"Whoever poisoned her probably used her current mug, then, and removed it after she died." Torin looked more closely at the body. "I must confess, I expected someone — larger."

That got a vicious smile out of Lisson. "Don't let her height fool you, Lieutenant. She may've been shorter'n most, but the Cap'n always felt like the tallest person on the deck. Nobody messed with her."

"Not twice, in any case." Chamblin had a smile of his own for that.

Those smiles fell at Torin's next words: "Well, nobody save whoever killed her."

"I assume," Danthres asked, "that you didn't put into port anywhere since you found the body?"

Chamblin was staring daggers at Torin, so Lisson replied. "We were three days out of Kalvar's Isle when Chamblin found her."

The gnome, meanwhile, moved menacingly toward Torin. "I won't have the Captain spoken of with disrespect."

"Neither respect nor disrespect was intended," Torin said tightly.

Danthres hastily added, "Our job here isn't to mourn the Pirate Queen, nor are we here to pass judgment on her—or on anyone else who didn't actually kill her. We are simply attempting to marshal facts in order to figure out who is responsible."

"To that end," Torin said before Chamblin could make a comment, "we will need to question your entire crew."

"I assume everyone is accounted for?" Danthres asked.

Lisson nodded. "We did a nose count, and found no one missing."

Danthres nodded. "So the killer is still on board."

"Or doesn't exist." Torin, for the first time since they arrived at the docks, looked pained. "Forgive me, but there is a possibility that must be considered—the poisoning could be self-inflicted."

Now Chamblin pulled out a dagger and moved toward Torin.

"Chamblin!" Lisson yelled.

"I will *not* have the Captain spoke of this way!"

Torin held up both hands. "Please, Chamblin, I—"

"Shut your shit-sucking mouth!"

Danthres said, "Chamblin you have one second to put that away or we will arrest you for assault on a member of the Castle Guard."

"You're welcome to try, halfbreed *bitch*!"

"Chamblin, stop being an idiot!" Lisson stepped between the quartermaster and Torin.

"Get out of my way, Lisson."

"This isn't the way to do this. The Cap'n deserves to have her murder *solved*. Besides, if she saw us squabbling like this…"

Taking his murderous gaze off Torin, Chamblin regarded Lisson with only slightly less anger. "She'd have us both swabbing the deck."

Lisson nodded. "Exactly. Now put the knife away." As Chamblin did so, the sailing master added, "Besides, she can't have killed herself. The mug is gone. Someone had to take that away."

"I'm afraid," Torin said, "that Chamblin's recent actions establish why that disproves nothing. He could have found the body and gotten rid of any evidence that pointed to suicide."

"I didn't," Chamblin said through gritted teeth. "I touched nothing in the room once I realized the Captain was dead."

"I don't suppose," Torin said slowly, "I could convince you to swear to that on the soul of Dwyte?"

Lisson's face fell; Danthres winced; Chamblin's dagger came back out. "How *dare* you!"

Before he could move forward, Lisson put a restraining hand on Chamblin's shoulder. "Easy, Chamblin, he doesn't know."

"My apologies if I've stepped on a custom," Torin said quickly. "I've only just learned of this oath."

Danthres said, "It's all right. One never requests the oath, Torin. It must be given voluntarily. If it's requested, it's meaningless."

"Again, my apologies, sir. I spoke out of ignorance of your customs." Torin bowed his head just before the ship bounced from the tide and he stumbled into the bulkhead.

To Danthres's relief, Chamblin notably shifted posture at Torin's use of the word "sir," as well as from the respectful tone in her partner's voice. Indeed, Torin was usually far more polite and deferential to witnesses than this, and she was glad to see it making a belated return.

"Apology accepted," Chamblin said as he sheathed the dagger.

"As is your word that you removed nothing from this room." Torin said that with another bow of his head.

"Thank you." Chamblin said. "I believe you mentioned something about talking to the crew? Our complement currently numbers forty-seven. Well—" He turned to look at the bed. "—forty-six now."

Danthres shot the quartermaster a look. "I remember each boat having at least seventy when I was a child."

"Times change," Chamblin said.

Lisson smiled. "We've grown more efficient with time. And many of our duties are reduced, as our reputation often precedes us, allowing us to perform our tasks with efficiency and dispatch."

"How fortunate for you." Torin had returned to the disdainful tone, to Danthres's annoyance.

She looked at him. "Twenty-three each?"

Torin nodded. "Do you have two rooms we might use?"

"Yes, of course." Lisson moved toward the door. "Come this way."

"You'll also need to dock the *Rising Jewel*," Danthres said.

Chamblin shook his head. "That's out of the question."

"I wasn't making a request, Chamblin." Danthres turned to face him and loomed over the gnome as much as she could—which was quite a bit, as she was tall even by the standards of her father's people, and Chamblin had the usual lack of height found in gnomes. "We need to make sure that nobody leaves the ship. The easiest way to do that is for you to dock and then we'll have Boneen magick the area around the ship—beyond the influence of the wards, but still surrounding them—to keep everyone on board."

"And also nearby for follow-up interviews," Torin added.

Proving to be utterly unintimidated by Danthres—disappointing her, as she prided herself on being able to scare the shit out of people on a regular basis—Chamblin said, "I'm sorry, that just isn't possible. There's too much risk in a port as crowded as Cliff's End."

"Fine, then we'll leave. Good luck to you." She moved toward the door where Torin was still standing.

"You can't leave!" Lisson cried.

"Watch us." Danthres stopped and turned to face him. "The Pirate Queen died at sea—you said you were, what, three days out of Kalvar's Isle?"

Lisson nodded.

"That," Torin said, "is well beyond the Castle Guard's jurisdiction. We would be completely within our rights to leave you alone."

"So if you want our help, you do things our way," Danthres said. "If you don't, then you may go ahead and sail on with a murderer on your boat."

An uncomfortable silence hung over the Pirate Queen's cabin for several seconds. But Danthres was firm in her demand. If nothing else, she was half convinced that the murderer had already leapt overboard since the nose count and they'd figure out who it was when that person didn't show up for an interview. In case that didn't happen, though, she wanted the *Rising Jewel* in dock.

Finally Chamblin said, "Sailing Master Lisson, would you be so kind as to set sail for the Cliff's End docks?"

"Bring her to the same spot you brought the dinghy," Danthres said. "That's the dock extension that's still under construction. It's a bit rough, but if you could handle the rocks and reefs by Sorlin, you can handle that. And it's enough away from the other boats that you should be left alone, especially once Boneen ensorcells you."

"If he can," Torin said. "Those are quite powerful wards."

"Then we'll put guards on the *Rising Jewel*. But I want you in dock and protected, and the murderer kept on board until we find whoever it is."

Lisson nodded and moved off to carry out Chamblin's order.

Torin looked at Chamblin. "Take us to where we may do our interviews, please?"

Chamblin let out a long breath and shook his head. "I don't like this."

"The Pirate Queen's been murdered," Danthres said softly. "I don't see how there would be anything to like."

SEVEN

Jaim sighed as she pushed open the door to the Dancing Seagull and found herself faced with wall to wall people.

It didn't used to be this way. Time was the Seagull didn't start getting seriously crowded until after sunset. Dockrats and sailors would head there for a night of hard drinking after a day of hard work.

Midafternoon, though, was usually—well, not *quiet*, but at least you could actually see the bar from the doorway, unlike now. Now, Jaim didn't even have any empirical proof the bar existed, blocked as it was by a sea of bodies.

Pushing her way through, she found herself at the far end of the bar, where Mom had, as usual, saved a seat.

"Hola, Mom."

"Hola, Jaim."

As she climbed onto the stool Mom had saved for him, a dwarf on the next stool muttered, "She *wasn't* lying. Amazing."

"Excuse me?" Jaim said.

Putting a hand on Jaim's arm, Mom said, "Leave it alone, Jaim."

However, Jaim was in a foul mood, and ignored her mother's advice. "You think my mother lied?"

"Place is packed," the dwarf said. "You shouldn't be takin' away seats from folks that wanna sit."

"Listen, you little—"

"Jaim." Mom spoke in her sternest tone.

When she was a girl, that tone always shut Jaim up, but she was in a really bad mood.

"My family has been coming to this bar every afternoon for almost two decades, dwarf."

The dwarf looked her up and down. "Came when you were an infant, did you?"

"Actually, yes. See, I run the fishing trawler the *Estarra*. I got it from Mom here and my Dad. It was called the *Feathered Wing* back then, but Mom renamed it after Dad died."

"I'm—I'm sorry." The dwarf sounded stunned. "Look, I just—"

"Every *single* day, our boat goes out there. It used to be just the two of them, then I went with when I was old enough. After Dad died, I took over." That part wasn't strictly speaking true. Mom went with Jaim for about a month after Dad died, before she realized that she didn't want to run the business without Dad, so she bequeathed it all to Jaim. But that part wasn't really the dwarf's business. "Every day, for all that time, the routine has been the same. Me and my crew board the *Estarra* and go out at sunup. We catch several netfuls of fish and bring them back to port just before midday. Then I go to Kala's Fish Emporium, she buys my catch, I split the take with my crew, and then I come here to have a drink with the very same mother you just accused of being a liar."

The dwarf seemed to be shrinking into his stool. "I *said* I was sorry."

"You said you were sorry my father died. I'm sorry, too. Because if he was still alive, he'd have pounded your fool head into the ground for talking shit about my mother."

Mom then added, "And he would've pounded *your* fool head into the ground for your foul language."

That broke through Jaim's foul mood, and she burst out with laughter.

Next to her, the dwarf tentatively laughed also, and said, "I'm sorry, truly, for any unkind thoughts I might have had. I actually buy my fish from Kala's, and if you're her source, you do good work."

"One of her sources," Jaim said. "Though you'd think by now she'd stop haggling. Every day it's the same—I name a price, we go back and forth for twenty minutes, and then she winds up buying the catch for the price I named in the first place."

Mom shook her head. "She's always been like that. I think she gets off on it or something."

Jaim reached for her drink, and realized it wasn't there. Glancing next to her, she saw that Mom didn't have a drink, either.

"Haven't you been served yet?"

Before Mom could even respond, the dwarf sipped his ale. "Been nursing this one for two hours. Damn bartender's too busy serving all the *bahrlans*."

"The what?" Jaim asked.

Mom was laughing. "It's a word in Ra-Telvish, it means 'filthy'."

"Elves ain't good for much," the dwarf said, "but they know how to craft an insult."

"C'mon, I doubt *all* these people are from Barlin," Jaim said.

"Been listenin' to 'em bitch and moan all day," the dwarf said. "Talkin' about the housing in New Barlin, talkin' about how hard it is to find work."

"Not just the *bahrlans*," Mom said. Jaim winced at her use of the slur. "Lots of locals having trouble finding work, too. Saw Abo on my way in here trollin' for work."

Jaim frowned. "I thought he was first mate on the *Breeze*."

"Yeah, he *was*. Brotherhood o' Wizards confiscated the boat, and now he ain't got nothin'. A year ago, they'd be linin' up to hire someone with his experience, but now there's too much experience, not enough boats."

"Experience? Pfah!" The dwarf slammed down his drink. "Barlin's landlocked, there's no 'experience' there at all. Nah, they're just takin' up all the cheap-shit sailor jobs, swabbin' decks and the like. And they take lower wages, too!"

"Well, when you've lost your home to a fire and are living in a strange city-state," Jaim said, "you're desperate enough to take any wage. Not surprised that captains're willing to pay less if the refugees are willing to take it."

"Shoulda gone to Iaron an' worked the mines, or bloody Velessa. Let the king an' queen deal with it, 'stead'a stickin' Lord Doofus on it."

The barkeep finally came over to them. "Sorry 'bout that, been crazy today. The usual?"

Mom nodded. "And make it snappy, will you please? It's not as if it's a surprise that my daughter and I are here in midafternoon."

"Sorry," the barkeep said again. "Still trying to get the hang of mixing a Prefarian Sunset."

The dwarf scowled. "What in Xinf's name is a Prefarian Sunset?"

"Popular drink in Barlin, apparently." The barkeep looked at the dwarf's almost-empty mug. "Another ale?"

"Sure, not like I'm goin' anywhere." The dwarf gulped down the rest of his ale and slammed the mug down on the bar.

"I've never seen you in here before," Jaim said.

"Usually go to the Joba's Arms, but that place is even *more* overrun with shit-sucking *bahrlans*. Figured I might get a lead on a job closer to the docks, but that ain't workin'. Ain't had any work since we finished New Barlin."

"You worked construction on Albinton?" Jaim asked.

The dwarf nodded. "Then once it was all done, I didn't have no more work. Came down here to try to work on the new dock construction, but all them jobs is taken — by *bahrlans*! I make their houses for 'em, then they go an' take my work away!"

The barkeep came back with three ales and put them in front of Jaim, Mom, and the dwarf. "Thanks," Jaim said.

"No problem."

"Hey, barkeep!" came a voice from further down the bar. "Three Prefarian Sunsets!"

"For Xinf's sake," the dwarf muttered.

Somebody else yelled, "Hey, why can't you *bahrlans* drink a *real* drink?"

"Excuse me?" the person who ordered the drinks said. Jaim couldn't quite make out who all was talking, as there were too many people. But the voices were shouting over the susurrus of noise in the packed bar.

"You heard me. In Cliff's End, we drink *real* drinks, not your Barlin shit."

Jaim winced, not liking where this was going.

"Oh, great," Mom muttered.

"What's wrong?" the dwarf asked.

"The main reason why we come here in the daytime is because the brawls usually happen at night."

Jaim shuddered as she gulped down a good third of her ale. The Dancing Seagull was famous for its late-night brawls, to the point where Mermaid Precinct usually had a patrol of night-shift guards standing near the bar around midnight every night just in case.

"Nah, this won't be a brawl."

The dwarf spoke with more confidence than Jaim had, as now she could see two people, one an elf, the other a human, pushing each other about halfway down the bar.

"Where do you get off callin' Barlin drinks shit, pointy-ears?"

Someone else cried out, "Barlin drinks *are* shit!"

"Nobody asked you!"

"His ears ain't even that pointy."

Jaim put her hand on Mom's wrist. "We should go."

"Yeah," Mom said.

"Oh, stop it, you two," the dwarf said. "It's just people blowin' off steam. Saw this in Joba's all the time. It'll bl—"

Before the dwarf could finish, he was interrupted by an ale mug colliding with his head.

"Ow!" he cried, putting his right hand to his right eye.

Jaim saw no transition. One second, people were standing around talking and drinking, the next arms and legs were flying, punches and mugs were being thrown, and it was utter chaos.

Quickly, Jaim hopped off her stool and crouched between it and Mom's stool. Mom did likewise between her stool and the wall. Jaim was very grateful that they had always sat in the corner of the bar—it was much easier to cower and stay out of the fighting.

A stool went flying overhead, crashing into the wall and shattering, splinters of wood flying about. Jaim raised her arms to shield her head from the debris.

Mom, who had done likewise, cried, "Nnnngh!"

"Let me see," Jaim said, reaching around the stool to take hold of Mom's arm.

There was a large splinter jutting from her forearm.

"Get it out, for Mitre's sake!" Mom cried.

Mom only invoked Mitre when she was in serious pain, so Jaim knew it was bad. She tugged at the splinter, and it came out.

Blood started pooling where her skin was cut, and Mom put her hand over it. "Dammit. This is out of hand."

"Yeah. I just hope it doesn't last too long, I want a healer to look at that arm."

"Let's get out of here alive, first."

Another mug went flying overhead, clattering to the floor after striking the wall.

Then, minutes later, it was all quiet, except for a lot of heavy breathing.

Hesitantly, Jaim rose from her squatting position to see what was happening.

People were slouched over tables, stools, and the bar itself. Others were sitting clutching limbs, bleeding, hyperventilating, and generally looking horrible. A few others were, like Jaim, sticking their heads out to see if it was safe.

One of those was the dwarf, who also had been hiding under one of the tables behind where he'd been sitting. He still had his right hand over his eye. "Xinf, this hurts," he was muttering.

The door flew open, and two guards with mermaid medallions etched into the chests of their leather armor came bursting in. "All right, that's enough!"

"Good timing," Jaim muttered.

Then someone screamed. Looking around, Jaim saw that it was the human from Barlin who was arguing with the elf.

"Soza's dead!"

One of the guards ran over to the human, and looked down at the floor.

"Yeah, he's dead all right," the guard said. Then he raised his voice. "Don't nobody even *think* about leavin' this bar! Yo, Jax, get one'a the youth squad to head to the castle and get some detectives down here. We got us a murder."

The other guard, Jax, nodded and headed to the door.

Jaim cried out, "And a healer, too!"

"Excuse me?" Jax asked.

"There are people here who are hurt, including my mother and my new friend here."

"Yeah, we'll take care of that," the first guard said.

Again, Jax nodded, and this time he left the premises.

"How long we gonna have to stay here?" Jaim asked.

"Till we say you can go. For now, sit tight."

Jaim sighed. She liked it better when it was quiet before the refugees—before the *bahrlans* came.

EIGHT

"I CAN'T BELIEVE SHE'S GONE."

Torin sighed. He'd spent the last several hours interviewing members of the Pirate Queen's crew in the galley, with a break only long enough to disembark as the *Rising Jewel* approached the docks. He went ahead in the dinghy with Lisson to tell Jayson and Gonzal to send for Boneen and to also get two more guards from Mermaid to keep people away from this section of the incomplete port extension. Only members of the Castle Guard and of the construction crews were to be allowed in.

After that, he'd gone back to questioning members of the crew, almost all of whom had started the interview the same way. This latest was a deck hand named Gavin.

"I'm afraid she is gone," Torin said as gently as he could—which was less so than it might have been had he not already expressed the same sentiments dozens of times already.

"Who would even *do* that? She was the finest captain that ever ran a boat."

"That is what we wish to find out. Having said that, I would think her list of enemies would be quite long."

"Yes, but they're all people who would attack *Rising Jewel* directly and try to kill all of us. Her enemies were foes of pirates, not of her personally. This was personal. And that doesn't make sense, because everyone who actually knew her as a person loved her."

Torin had to admit to being impressed. This Gavin fellow seemed to have given this some thought, which put him one up on most of the rest of the crew. They were all just devastated at the loss and didn't really think past that.

"It is my experience," Torin said after a moment, "that nobody is loved by everybody."

"Then you never met the Captain. She was amazing."

Torin leaned forward on the bench, elbows on the table while facing Gavin, who sat on the bench opposite. "No, but I saw the results of her actions. The people who didn't get food because she raided a convoy. The soldiers who were forced to go into battle with substandard equipment because she stole from a sword distributor. The places of business that had to close because their supplier was raided. There are, I'm quite sure, plenty who have gone to bed cursing her name and woke up the next morning doing the same."

Gavin folded his arms defiantly. "Perhaps, Lieutenant, but they were none of them on this ship. And were those hypothetical people you mention here before me, I would show them the starving children we fed with the food from that convoy, the rebels who fought tyrants with the weapons from that sword distributor, the alcohol we supplied to healers trying to aid the war-ravaged that we took from those inns."

Torin smiled. "I never mentioned inns, but your point is well taken. However, my point still stands—not everyone is necessarily going to think highly of the Pirate Queen."

"Perhaps. But as I said, Lieutenant, everyone on this boat was devoted to her. We all loved her and would die for her."

With a sigh, Torin said, "So you've no idea who might have poisoned her?"

"I'm sorry, Lieutnenant. I mean, everyone had access to the rat poison, so it could've been anybody—but it also couldn't have been anybody on this ship. Look, I've only been here a year, and I'd die for the Captain. And us new recruits are the ones with the weakest loyalty to her—most of the people serving on *Rising Jewel* have been with her for years, decades even. Nobody on this boat wanted her dead."

"You said, 'us new recruits.' Who else is new?"

"Oh, four of us came on board all at once about a year ago. We lived in Sorlin, you see, but the community disbanded."

"You're from Sorlin?" That surprised Torin.

Gavin nodded. "Rodolfo, the boatswain, he invited anyone who wanted to join the Captain's crew to come with him, and three of us took him up on it."

"Hm." Torin rubbed his chin. "Very well, Gavin, thank you for your time."

"Goodness, is that you, Danthres?"

Looking up in shock at the familiar voice, Danthres saw the tall, wiry form of Rodolfo enter the wardroom. He was much more muscular than he was when Danthres had last seen him, and had grown a rather large mustache, but it was definitely him. She recognized the twinkle in his black eyes instantly, as well as the lilt in his resonant voice.

Like Danthres herself, Rodolfo was half-elf and half-human, but the only evidence of his elven heritage was his height and slightly tapered ears. Otherwise, his dark coloring, dark eyes, and flat chin made him look completely human.

"Rodolfo?" She stood up and did something she never did with an interview subject in fifteen years in the Castle Guard: she hugged him.

"What are you doing on a pirate ship?" she asked during the embrace.

"What are you doing in guard armor?"

She pulled away. "My job. After I—I left Sorlin, I eventually found my way to Cliff's End. I'm a senior detective now, and Lisson specifically—"

Holding up a hand, Rodolfo said, "I know, I was there for the arguments."

"Arguments?" Danthres sat back down in the wardroom chair and indicated that Rodolfo should do likewise in the chair opposite her.

"Chamblin was against bringing in outsiders. Lisson pointed out that none of us knew how to investigate a murder, plus everyone on the boat was a suspect." Rodolfo smiled sheepishly at that. "They almost came to blows over that. Everyone wanted to kill whoever was responsible, but we couldn't imagine who that was." He sighed. "It was that last part that made the difference. We had absolutely no notion as to who might have done this. It just didn't make sense."

"Not even the newest arrivals?"

Rodolfo smiled, and he had the same mischievous smile as an adult that he'd had when he was yet another half-breed infant the Pirate Queen had brought to Sorlin for refuge. Though even then, Danthres knew he was special.

"I'm one of the newest arrivals," he said.

"And already a boatswain?"

"I had the experience. I originally left Sorlin when I was a teenager and signed aboard a merchant ship, *Letashia*. Unfortunately..." He trailed off.

"Go on."

After taking a deep breath, he said, "We got caught in that hurricane a few years ago. Letashia was demolished, and only a few of us survived."

"I'm sorry," Danthres said, and she meant it. It was never easy to lose comrades and friends. Danthres has lost far too many over the years, from her best friend Lil in Sorlin to the servant girl Harra in Treemark to so many fellow detectives who perished on the job, the latest of whom was Hawk. It never got easier.

But those years of experience also taught her that the words of others were often useless, so she limited herself to simply saying she was sorry, acknowledging the person's sadness without making the whole thing ridiculous with platitudes.

"Thank you," Rodolfo said. "I didn't really know what to do with myself, so I came back to Sorlin. I only left last year when the community disbanded—I assume you heard about that?"

Danthres nodded. "Javian visited on his way to Saptor Isle last year and filled me in."

Rodolfo brightened. "Oh, so you two are speaking again?"

Wincing, Danthres said, "After a fashion. We've been writing each other." That reminded Danthres that she owed him a letter. She also realized that she had broken her cardinal rule that she was the only one who asked questions during an interview.

Of course, Rodolfo *was* an old friend...

"So you signed on to the *Rising Jewel* after leaving Sorlin?"

Nodding, Rodolfo said, "Yes, along with Gavin and Nimma, two of the deck hands, and Bottin, the carpenter's mate."

Danthres didn't recognize the first two names, but she knew the third well. "Wait, Bottin?"

"Yes."

"She couldn't build a rabbit snare, with step-by-step instructions."

Rodolfo grinned. "Which is why she's the carpenter's *mate*. She's the apprentice, and she's learning."

"How's that coming along?"

Tilting his head, Rodolfo said, "Slowly. Our carpenter is very patient."

"He'd have to be." Danthres shook her head and chuckled. Bottin always broke everything she touched, much less anything she tried to build. "So you four are the newest arrivals?"

"And Cook. He wasn't from Sorlin, but he signed on at the same time we did. I think he's from Treemark."

"Voran." Danthres had spoken to him earlier, but he'd said more or less the same things everyone else had said. He also sounded more like he was from one of the more northern city-states — Barlin, Iaron, or Cliff's End itself — than from Tremark. "And he seemed utterly devastated by the Captain's death."

"The Captain always made it a point to treat Cook well." He chuckled. "I have to admit, I didn't know his name was Voran until you said it just now. He was always just 'Cook.'"

"And the Captain was always the Captain. Or the Pirate Queen."

"Actually, her real name was Lillyana. She told me once, about six months ago. We'd just salvaged a boat that had hit the Zokorvian Reefs, and in gratitude, they gave us a case of wine. We put in on Vikeez Isle and celebrated."

"Please tell me you didn't try to throw a virgin into the volcano."

Rodolfo looked at her as if she had lost her mind. "I'm sorry?"

Danthres shook her head. "Never mind. Had a case involving virgins and the Vikeez volcano over midwinter."

"Oh. Well, no, the volcano is still inactive, and virgin-free as far as I could determine."

"Good to hear."

"But we celebrated on the beach that night, and at one point, the Captain, who was on her fourth bottle of wine, very drunkenly declared that she had been reluctant to take me on board at first, but that now she was glad to have me as boatswain. I said, 'Thank you very much, Captain,' and she said, 'My name is Lillyana.' And, ah, and then she passed out."

Danthres found that to be very interesting, though probably not for the reasons Rodolfo thought.

"All right, I think that's all we need for now. We may have more questions. For now, you're all confined to the boat until we find the killer."

"That makes sense." Rodolfo stood up. "Thank you, Danthres. And perhaps when this is over we can share a meal and catch up more properly?"

"I'd like that." Danthres smiled, memories of Rodolfo arriving in Sorlin as an infant, of the sweet child she and Lil sometimes took care of, of the cocksure teenager he had just turned into when she was thrown out of Sorlin, all came crashing into her mind. "But first let's find out who killed the Captain."

"Yes, of course."

TORIN FOUND DANTHRES WAITING FOR HIM ON THE DECK, ALONG WITH Lisson and a tall, mustachioed sailor Torin didn't recognize. He had tapered ears and was tall enough to indicate elven blood in his heritage, so he might have been one of the other Sorlin refugees Gavin mentioned.

The *Rising Jewel* was now anchored near the under-construction new port. It wasn't ready to actually house a boat, but it was close enough. Torin could see Boneen standing on the deck. He could also see Jayson, Gonzal, and about a half-dozen other guards from Mermaid, many of whom were keeping back the crowd that was building.

"I see the *Jewel* has drawn some attention."

"Yes," Lisson said souly. "It's why we prefer not to dock in large ports. It only causes a scene."

Danthres was peering at the dock. "Is that Mannit?"

Torin followed her gaze, and saw a guard in a green cloak. It was too far away to be completely sure, but Mannit was the day-shift sergeant for Mermaid Precinct. "Not surprising. Mannit always prefers to be out and about instead of staying at the precinct. He'd rather be in the action."

"Mmm." Danthres turned to face Lisson. "I take it that all the crew remains accounted for?"

"No one left the boat after the last nose count, no," Lisson said. "Same people've been here since we set sail last."

"Good. You'll need to stay put. Torin and I will return to the castle, report to our captain, and compare notes on our interviews. We will likely have to follow up with some of your crew—if so, we'll summon them to the castle."

"All right," Lisson said. "I'll take you back in the dinghy."

"May I make a suggestion?" the tall man asked.

Lisson shrugged in response. "Go ahead, Rodolfo."

Torin nodded. It *was* one of the Sorlin refugees. Danthres seemed to be looking upon him with a certain kindness as he spoke. Torin had chalked that up to Lisson's presence as an old friend, but it might well have applied to both of them. He made a mental note to ask Danthres how many of the Sorlin quartet that signed on last year she was familiar with.

"Since we'll be stuck in port in any case, let's give the crew something to do. I think we should do a thorough search of *Rising Jewel* to find a stowaway."

Looking at the boatswain as if he were mad, Lisson asked incredulously, "A stowaway?"

"It makes sense," Danthres said. "We're assuming one of the crew did it, because the boat is a closed environment, but what if it was someone who snuck on board for the purpose of killing the Captain?"

"Wouldn't they have gone overboard after doing the deed?" Lisson asked.

"Wouldn't we have noticed that?" Rodolfo asked right back.

"Perhaps." Lisson shook his head. "But I can think of several ways one could sneak off-ship without the lookouts noticing or the wards being activated. Still, the notion is absurd. We haven't had a stowaway in almost a decade."

Torin said gently, "You haven't had your captain killed before. I don't think precedent should be your watchword at this stage."

"Besides," Rodolfo said, "the point is more to give the crew a task to perform while we sit in this port waiting for the lieutenants to solve the case. It would be a useful distraction."

Lisson rubbed his chin and scratched his head, then nodded. "Very well, Boatswain. Since it was your idea, you can organize it. And who knows? Perhaps we will turn up a stowaway."

"Aye aye, Sailing Master."

"But first, let's get Danthres and her partner back to shore." Lisson moved toward the dinghy —

— and then he stopped just as he was about to climb over the deck railing and onto the dinghy, which was tied to the rigging. "I can't move forward!"

Torin sighed. He'd been afraid of that. "Boneen has already warded the area around the *Jewel*. If he's done it right, Danthres and I should be able to pass through them, but nobody else currently on board will. For what it's worth, that would include any stowaways."

Rodolfo smiled. "Good to know."

"Get started on the search, Rodolfo," Lisson said. "I'll lower the dinghy."

Torin had no trouble clambering over the railing onto the dinghy, and neither did Danthres, so Boneen got that part right. Though, he did feel the same shiver that he'd felt when he'd boarded the boat earlier.

Within a few minutes, they'd managed to maneuver the dinghy to the port, where Gonzal grabbed the rope and secured it to the dock.

"Thank you," Torin said to the M.E., "for putting the wards in place."

"You should thank me," Boneen said in his crankiest tone — even more so than usual, which was impressive. "It was *incredibly* difficult. The wards they've already emplaced on that ship are almost palpable. I understand now why you didn't ask for a peel-back."

"The wards are apparently necessary," Torin said.

Danthres looked at Gonzal. "This dinghy is to remain secured here. We may need to come back or send someone else to fetch people and bring them to the castle for more questioning." She turned to Boneen. "The wards will allow anyone from the Castle Guard on board, yes?"

Boneen reached into his satchel. "Yes, but if you wish to bring someone off the boat, you'll need to carry this." He pulled a red crystal out. "No, wait, that's not the right one. Hang on." He rummaged through it, then pulled out a purple one. "If you're carrying this charm, then anyone you're touching can also penetrate the wards."

Gonzal took the purple crystal. "What happens if I let go while we're going through?"

"I would advise very strongly against finding that out," Boneen said. "Now if you'll excuse me, this entire enterprise has been utterly exhausting." He gestured and disappeared in a flash of light.

"I wish he'd taken us with him." Torin gazed with trepidation at the crowd that had gathered to gape at the *Rising Jewel*.

"That makes one of us." Danthres shuddered.

Torin knew that Danthres always threw up whenever she was the subject of a Teleport Spell. "Looking at that crowd, I suspect that if given a choice between moving through it and puking, I would choose the latter."

Danthres regarded him with amused amazement. "*Have* you ever puked in your life, Torin?"

"Oh, yes." Unbidden, memories of his first winter away from Myverin came back to him. He got very ill, and kept heaving long after the meager contents of his stomach had been upchucked back to the earth, as it were.

Mannit saw them and came over, his green cloak billowing behind him in the sea breeze. There were still half a dozen guards keeping the crowd at bay. "How long these shitbrains gonna be in dock?"

Danthres said, "Until we figure out which of the forty-six people on board is a murderer."

Glancing back at the crowd. "Well, make it quick, will you please? I already got a murder in the Seagull, and now this. Crowd control was already *outta* control before today, and now it's gonna be a helluva lot worse."

"Wait," Danthres said, "someone got murdered in the Seagull—in *daylight*?"

"First time for everything, right?" Mannit said with a grim chuckle.

"Who caught the case?" Danthres asked. "Manfred and Kellan?"

The sergeant shook his head. "No, Aleta and that half-dwarf."

Torin grinned. "No guarantee of success, then."

"Oh, please," Danthres said, "you're not putting stock in their stupid streak, are you?"

"They *have* closed a dozen cases in a row."

"So what?"

"We've never closed a dozen in a row."

Danthres rolled her eyes. "Because they always give us the difficult cases. A copper says they don't make it to thirteen."

"You're on." Torin glanced back at the *Rising Jewel*. "Of course, they didn't give us this one, either, it was dropped on us."

"Hope it ain't *that* difficult," Mannit said. "Look, do us a favor—see if Dru can send down a few guards from the other precincts to help out with crowd control? It's gonna be a mess here tonight, especially if the Seagull can't open back up."

"We will," Torin said. "If you could ask the guards you do have to help clear us a path?"

The pair of them headed toward the crowd, joined by Mannit and Gonzal. The guards from Mermaid were able to clear a thin path, and the two lieutenants managed to squeeze through the docks and work their way to Salmon Alley, which would lead them across to Meerka Way.

Once they could walk side by side instead of single file, Danthres asked Torin, "So now that we're away from the crew, I can ask this: what is it you have against pirates?"

Evasively, Torin asked, "What makes you think—"

But Danthres, typically, wouldn't let him get away with being evasive. "Don't give me that. You've been snotty about pirates from the moment we started talking to Lisson. You haven't been this terse and obnoxious since your father visited last year."

All things considered, he would have preferred not to annoy his partner, but that seemed a forlorn hope. "I'm sorry, I know they're your friends, but—" He sighed. "I don't like pirates. I encountered several of them during the war—not the Pirate Queen herself, mind, but a few others. Not many, as they mostly stayed out of it."

"So what's the problem?"

Another sigh. "They mostly stayed out of it. They claimed to have no loyalty to any nation, to be a people of their own, but mostly that struck me—and several of my fellow soldiers—as an excuse to avoid having to get involved in the war. And when they *did* get involved, they would attack our supply lines, leaving us without necessary food and materiel. They either ignored the war or exploited it for their own benefit, and I have very little use for that."

"They didn't just do that—or, at least, the Captain didn't," Danthres said as they turned onto Meerka Way, heading away from the sea toward the castle. "She broke the blockade any number of times in order to rescue orphans and mixed-blood children who were condemned to death and bring them to Sorlin."

"Like Rodolfo, Gavin, Bottin, and Nimma?" Torin grabbed at the opening to yank the conversation back to the actual case.

Danthres nodded. "Yes, though the only ones I knew from my time there were Rodolfo and Bottin."

That conveniently answered Torin's question from when he was questioning Gavin. "Have they changed much?"

"I always knew Rodolfo would do well in whatever he chose to do. He was always very intelligent and self-directed." She smiled. "But then, he came by that honestly."

"What do you mean?"

Danthres hesitated. "Rodolfo is the Pirate Queen's son."

NINE

"This is exciting," Dannee said as she and Aleta worked their way through the late-afternoon crowds on Meerka Way. "I've never even *been* to the docklands before."

Aleta shot her a look. "What? How's that possible?"

Dannee shrugged. "I came here from Barlin on a caravan. Then I found lodgings in Dragon Precinct, and I got hired and was assigned to Unicorn Precinct. The farthest from the castle I've ever gone is to Jorbin's Way."

"So not much of a fish eater?" Aleta asked with a smile. The main reason why anyone went to the docks was if you had business with one of the boats or wanted to buy fish.

Dannee's nose wrinkled. "Xinf, no, I can't *stand* fish. Awful stuff."

"Prepare yourself, then," Aleta said as they crossed Jorbin's Way, bringing them into new territory for the half-dwarf. "By the time we hit the River Walk, all you're going to smell is fish."

To Aleta's amusement, Dannee wrinkled her nose the moment they crossed the River Walk. "This is *really* horrible."

"You get used to it."

"How?"

Aleta chuckled.

They arrived at the Dancing Seagull. A large crowd was gathered around, barely held in check by three guards, Lavian, Kass, and Jax.

People were grumbling.

"When we gonna get to go in?"

"Oh, shit, the Cloaks are here."

"Need me a *drink* f'Wiate's sake!"

"Me bruvver's in 'ere! Need t'see 'im!"

Ignoring them, Aleta walked up to Lavian. "Hello, Fran."

"Aleta. Sorry, *Lieutenant*." Lavian grinned at that. "An' hey, you must be Ocly. Congrats."

Dannee's nose was still wrinkled. "Thanks. Does it smell better inside?"

"Better than *what*, exactly?" Lavian turned to Aleta. "We'll keep the hordes back, but you may wanna get a move on. They're gettin' ugly."

"Shouldn't we summon the magickal examiner?" Dannee asked.

Jax said, "I sent for 'im when I asked for you two an' a healer. But he sent a mage-bird sayin' he was busy with somethin' involvin' a pirate ship?"

Dannee nodded. "Lieutenant Tresyllione and Lieutenant ban Wyvald's case."

Aleta sighed. "Of course, the so-called 'senior detectives' get use of the M.E. over us."

Then she shoved the door to the Seagull open only to find a huge crowd of people. Filbert was standing near the bar, several people were sitting at various tables, grumbling to themselves and looking very uncomfortable, and a healer was in the corner, treating the arm of a human woman.

Dannee said, "But their case involves the Pirate Queen, doesn't it? She's kind of important. And besides, they *are* the senior detectives."

"That was just an excuse to give them a pay raise for being in the Guard so long without a promotion."

"Yes, but look around." Dannee indicated the tavern with her hand. "The peel-back needs to be in a space with no living creatures in it. What are we supposed to do with all of them?"

With a sigh, Aleta said, "That's true." Mostly she just wanted to be cranky at Tresyllione, but that was unfair, and mostly out of habit. Torin and the half-breed were really good at their jobs, and Aleta had to admit that working with them the past year had taught her a lot about being a detective. She and Tresyllione had even worked together and put a couple of cases down, starting with the lothHanthra murder.

But she still didn't *like* Tresyllione, and took a certain pleasure in being angry at her.

In this case, though, Dannee was right. She counted upwards of a hundred people in this tavern, and they needed to interview all of them, which meant keeping them *in* the tavern. That would take hours, so there was no point in even summoning Boneen until then.

"Besides," Dannee said with a smile, "with all these witnesses, I'm sure *someone* saw who did it."

That comment made it much easier for Aleta to believe that Dannee had never set foot in Mermaid before. Witnesses tended to mind their own business and remain tight-lipped on the docks.

She walked over to Filbert. "Everyone still here?"

Filbert winced. "Can't guarantee that. By the time Jax and I got here, the body'd already dropped. I can tell you that nobody's left since we arrived."

The healer, a dwarven woman, wandered over to the detectives. "Excuse me, are you in charge?"

"I'm Lieutenant Aleta lothLathna, and I'm in charge of this investigation, yes."

"Good, then you can pay me."

"Um…" Aleta stammered. "That's not my—"

The dwarf held up a hand. "Please don't tell me it's not your department. The Castle Guard owes me eleven silver from the last three times I healed people at one of your crime scenes. I used to get paid regularly, but the last year or so, it's taken forever! Now I've treated seven people here, so that's another seven silver, so you now owe me eighteen!"

"I, uh—"

Dannee stepped forward. "I'm sorry, it's been such a pain, hasn't it? It's all because of Lord Albin dying. You see his son, Lord Blayk, he instituted a new accounting system, and Lord Doval has kept it intact. It takes forever for bills to be paid now, and it's all because of the stupid guilds. They kept not billing properly or paying properly and money kept getting misplaced and lost, and so Lord Blayk put in this new system and *we* have to pay for it. It's been how long since one of your bills was paid?"

"A month."

Nodding, Dannee said, "That's about right. You should get the next one soon—it's been taking about a month lately, because there's been such a backlog, what with all the new construction contracts for the docks and for New Barlin."

The healer shook her head. "Stupid shitbrains in the castle—don't they know that us normal folk have bills to pay?"

"It's been my experience," Aleta said, "that the upper classes rarely give normal folk any thought whatsoever."

"At least," Dannee added, "until tax time comes around."

That got the healer to laugh. "That's the truth, as Xinf is my witness." She sighed. "All right, thank you."

Aleta asked, "How badly were people hurt?"

"Honestly, it wasn't that bad—just some scrapes and gashes and such. I've been to brawls that have been much worse in this very tavern. Well—" She hesitated, then indicated the corpse on the floor with her head. "—except for that."

After the healer left, Aleta turned to Dannee. "I wasn't aware that there was a new billing system."

Dannee smile brightly under her beard. "There isn't. I just wanted to get her to leave without raising a fuss."

"You were right about one thing," Filbert said. "My cousin's in charge of one of the construction crews for New Barlin, and they're way behind on gettin' paid."

Aleta's respect for her new partner had just gone up a notch. "All right, do we know who our victim is?"

"Name's Soza Lambit. Lives in New Barlin, came to Cliff's End 'long with everyone else."

"How'd you get that much information?"

Filbert pointed at a human standing nearby. "That's his brother, Ditha Lambit."

For a moment, Aleta stared at the brother. "Keep him here. I want to talk to him last, after I've heard from everyone else. Let's start talking to all the other witnesses so we can get them out of here so Boneen can cast the peel-back, if he ever shows up. If we're lucky, one of them saw something—and if we're even luckier, one of them will be willing to share."

Now Dannee sounded confused. "Why wouldn't they be willing to share?"

Filbert actually burst out laughing at that, and then stopped when he saw the hurt look on Dannee's face. "Wait—that was a serious question?"

"She's never been to Mermaid before," Aleta said by way of explanation to Filbert, then turned to Dannee, whose respect just lost that notch. "This isn't Unicorn, Dannee. The people here aren't civic-minded, they're working folk who just want to live their lives and not get involved."

"That's madness."

"That's life on the docks. And in Goblin, for that matter, and most of Dragon. Like I said to the healer, the folks in the castle don't care about regular people, and the feeling is very mutual—and to them, *we're* the folks in the castle." She turned to Filbert and pointed to the corner of the tavern nearest the door. "I'm going to sit in that corner. Dannee, you take that corner over there." She pointed at the opposite corner. "Bring one person at a time to each of us and let them go when we're done."

Filbert nodded. "And the brother's last?"

"Yes."

Aleta then headed over to the corner she'd indicated and steeled herself for a litany in selective blindness. She was not disappointed.

"Didn't see a thing."

"No idea what happened."

"I think somebody hit somebody else. Not sure."

"I was just drinkin' an' then everyone was fightin'. Dunno what started it."

"People were yelling and then I hid under the table."

And on and on.

But some people's blindness was leavened with anger.

"It was probably those *bahrlans*."

Aleta winced at the mangling of her native tongue. In Ra-Telvish, *bahrlan* was an adjective, not a noun. "Filthy what?"

"No, I mean the people from Barlin."

"You call them *bahrlans*?"

The witness nodded. "It doesn't surprise me that they'd go 'round killin' each other. Buncha shits who shoulda stayed in where they belong. Stupid *bahrlans*."

Aleta heard that term several more times throughout the interviewing process.

"This used to be a great place to come in the daytime. Then the *bahrlans* all started showing up. I'm glad one of 'em's dead, maybe now they'll go drink somewhere else."

"It was someone arguing with a *bahrlan* over those shitty drinks they always order."

"The damn *bahrlans* were all over the place. I couldn't even order a drink, there were so many of them."

"I don't even know why I come here anymore. All I see is these damn refugees from Barlin. I'm sorry he's dead, but I'm not sur-

prised. Those people are just asking for it with the way they be-
have."

"They're just bargin' in here all'a time, makin'a mess'a things. Not
surprised one of them got their fool selves killed."

It wasn't until the interviews were almost finished that she actually
managed to get something resembling a fact.

"So there was these three bahrlans, right? An' they ordered themselves some stupid *bahrlan* drink. Poofer Sunrise or some nonsense."

"Prefarian Sunset?" Aleta asked.

"That was it, yeah. So they order the drinks, right? An' some
shitbrain asks why they can't drink a real drink, right? An' they start
yellin' at each other an' then they start pushin' each other, right?
And then I get hit in the head, so I don't know what happened after
that."

"Did you see who started the fight?"

"I dunno who they were, right? One was an elf, one was a human,
but I ain't seen much besides that. 'Specially after I got hit inna head,
right?"

The next witness was a young human woman. "How much longer
do my mother and I have to stay here?"

"As long as this interview takes. And the one with your mother."

"She's talking to your partner."

Aleta glanced over and saw an older woman who bore a resemblance to the woman she was interviewing talking with Dannee. "Then
you'll be out of here sooner. What's your name?"

"Jaim."

"Do you know what happened?"

"Not exactly. There was an elf and a human pushing each other
after one of them ordered one of those *bahrl*— one of those Barlin
drinks."

Heartened by Jaim's decision to not use the slur, Aleta asked, "And
then what happened?"

"I've no idea. The person next to me got hit in the head with a mug,
and then Mom and I hid under the bar stools until it was over."

"Do you know what the fight was about?"

"A drink, I think. Look, my Mom and I have been coming here since
I was a little girl. It's never been this bad before. You lot have to do
something about it."

"Like what?"

Jaim shrugged. "I don't know! Get rid of the stupid *bahrlans*! They're the ones causing all this trouble."

Finally, with all the other witnesses taken care of, Aleta called Dannee over and they sat down with Ditha Lambit.

"My brother and I were just sitting at the bar, minding our own business," Ditha said. "We were drinking, talking about where we'd go to look for work tomorrow."

"What kind of work?" Dannee asked.

"We just finished a job hauling cargo for the *Dekird*, but it's sailed off for Saptor, so we need to find more work." He glanced over at his brother's body. "Well, I do. I guess. After I deal with that. For Temisa's sake, I can't believe he's dead."

"So you were drinking and talking about work...?" Aleta prompted.

Ditha shuddered a bit. "Right, yes. Someone walked up to the bar from the back of the tavern. I thought I recognized him from around the neighborhood. He ordered three Prefarian Sunsets, so I knew he was from Barlin also. I was about to ask him something when this elf started yelling at him. They started shoving each other, and then the next I know, everyone was beating each other up. I hid under a bar stool, and Soza did the same." Ditha wiped tears from his eyes. "After it was over, I got up, but Soza didn't. He was on the floor, dead." He started crying.

Dannee stood up and put an arm around him. "It's okay, Mr. Lambit. We'll find out who killed him."

Aleta winced. It didn't do to make such promises. Well, unless you were Manfred and Kellan and could apparently solve any case that came your way. Absent that, this was going to be a hard one to crack, unless the peel-back told them something useful.

"Th-thank you, Lieutenant."

"We don't have any more questions," Aleta said as she rose to her feet. "We'll take care of the body and let you know when you can make arrangements."

"There's—there's no arrangements to be made. His soul is with Temisa now, and I don't care what happens to his body."

"Right." Aleta had always had trouble keeping track of the different death rituals of the various religions of the people of Flingaria. She herself didn't believe in any of them. The only higher power she'd seen any evidence of were wizards, and they certainly weren't worth worshipping. None of the other beings she'd heard so many invoke—

Wiate, Xinf, Ghandurha, Mitre, Temisa, and the others—were ones she had any proof of the existence of. "We also may have further questions," she added as Ditha headed to the door.

"Of course. Thank you, Lieutenants."

Finally, Aleta went over to look at the body, which she preferred to do with the tavern now cleared out. She knelt down next to it and looked the corpse over. "He was strangled."

Dannee stood next to her, and her eyes went wide. "How can you tell *that*?"

Pointing at the victim's neck, Aleta said, "You can see the impressions of the fingers. Also look at his eyes."

Nose scrunching the way it had when she'd smelled fish, Dannee said, "I'd rather not."

"When people are strangled, their eyes get red. I've seen it before."

"When you—um—" Dannee hesitated.

Aleta stood straight. "When I killed people for the Shranlaseth?"

"Um, well, yes."

"It's all right, Dannee, I don't mind talking about it. I did kill people, yes, and when I strangled them, this is what they looked like."

"I guess that's useful? Investigating deaths when you know so many ways to kill people?"

"It's come in handy."

Filbert had gone outside for a moment, and walked back in.

Upon seeing him, Aleta said, "Filbert, can you get a detail together to bring the victim's body back to Boneen's lair in the castle?"

"Me an' Jax can do it. But you need to open the tavern back up."

"Why's that?"

"'Cause Fran and Kass just got sent to the docks to help Mannit with crowd control."

Aleta frowned. "Why are there crowds on the docks that need controlling?"

"Pirate Queen's ship is in dock. Well, in the new docks they're buildin', anyhow. There's gapers, so Sarge needs help to keep 'em back."

"Wonderful." Aleta knew intellectually that she was more angry because that was Tresyllione's case, but it was still annoying. "But we can't reopen the tavern, the M.E. will have to—"

But Filbert was shaking his head. "Mannit said Boneen teleported his tiny ass back to the castle after he was done doing whatever it was he was doing to the Pirate Queen's boat to keep 'em in place."

Aleta sighed and repeated, "Wonderful."

"Can't he just teleport back?" Dannee asked.

Shaking her head, Aleta said, "If Boneen teleports from a crime scene, it means he's going to take a nap as soon as he arrives in his little sanctum in the castle basement. We won't be hearing from him again until tomorrow."

"Okay," Dannee said, "then we'll figure out a way to clear out the tavern tomorrow when he's awake!"

"Perhaps." She looked at her partner. "What did your interviews tell you?"

"Well, you're right about people not wanting to get involved. Several of the witnesses obviously saw something but just as obviously didn't want to tell me anything about it. And a lot of them just said *awful* things about my fellow Barlin natives."

"So did a lot of my interviews. But no indication of who did it?"

"No. I mean, an elf and a human got into a shouting match, but it wasn't even the victim who was part of that."

"It was probably just someone using the brawl as cover." Aleta sighed. "And it was definitely personal."

"Why do you say that?"

"Because he was strangled. If you're killing someone because you want them killed quickly or efficiently, especially in a situation like this, the last thing you want to do is strangle them, as it takes several minutes. But it's also very up-close and personal—you're using your hands and you're on top of the victim and watching as they die slowly."

"You—you know a lot about this." Dannee sounded somewhat revolted.

"Killing was my job for a very long time. I take my jobs very seriously." She sighed. "All right, Filbert get the body out of here and then let them open back up. We'll figure out a way to get Boneen to do the peel-back tomorrow."

"You got it."

TEN

DANTHRES STILL REMEMBERED THE DAY THE CAPTAIN BROUGHT RODOLFO TO Sorlin.

It was not long after the Elf Queen had wiped out the western elves, approximately a year before the attack on Umrig's Pass led to the declaration of war between the elves and the human-dwarf alliance.

The Captain had arrived with her ship and had brought refugees to Sorlin, as she had many times before.

But this was the first time she was carrying one of the refugees in her arms.

Danthres had been walking with Elsthar Javian and his mother Sharrastha, who had been Danthres's mother in all but blood as well. They were debating over what to have for dinner that night when Tharri saw the *Rising Jewel.*

Sharrastha had gone to alert the council that the Pirate Queen had arrived, while Danthres had gone with Tharri to meet the dinghy from the *Rising Jewel* at the port.

The Captain had been younger then, her large dark eyes and lustrous black hair even more striking. Her sailing master was piloting the boat, and there were several people who obviously were halfbreeds.

The boy in the Captain's arms was the only infant.

After they secured the dinghy, Sharrastha returned with several other people from Sorlin to help guide the refugees in.

Tharri and Danthres went to the Captain. "It's been quite a while. We were wondering if you'd ever see you again."

The Captain smiled brightly. Later in life, many of the stories Danthres would hear about the Pirate Queen were that she never smiled, and perhaps she didn't when she was on the open seas, but in Sorlin she was always relaxed.

"We've been busy—we spent the better part of the last ten months in hiding from the Elf Queen's navy. She got it in her head that we were aiding the western elves."

"Were you?" Danthres asked.

The smile broadened. "Of course we were, Thressa." Then the smile fell. "For all the good it did. We were forced into hiding and only just now came out. But our first trip was to elf country, and as you can see, our labors were fruitful. Most of these people were condemned to death." She held out the boy. "And then there's little Rodolfo here. The purity squads haven't gotten to him yet, but it's only a matter of time."

Tharri took the infant in his arms, for which Danthres was grateful, as she hated dealing with infants.

For her part, she looked into the dinghy. "Didn't Kerestha come with you?" The elf had been the sailing master on the *Rising Jewel*'s sister ship, the *Heart of Silver*, but he often came with her to visit Sorlin. Besides which, Danthres was fairly certain that the Captain and Kerestha were having a secret relationship, and she'd been looking forward to teasing both of them about it.

But then she saw the sad look on the Captain's face, and realized she should perhaps have not brought it up.

"I'm afraid Kerestha was a victim of the Elf Queen's attempt at vengeance against us. We lost him along with Hiram, Marta, and Gibranig at Thanthrak's Peak."

"I'm sorry," Tharri said. "Come, let's get Rodolfo settled with the others."

The Captain's smile returned. "I doubt he'll comprehend the usual arrival talk about not being disruptive, though you're welcome to try."

Tharri chuckled. "At the very least, I should wait for him to wake up."

By the time Danthres finished telling Torin the story, they had reached the castle. The story itself had been interrupted numerous times by having to wade through the crowds on Meerka Way through Goblin and Dragon Precincts, especially at the intersection with Boulder Pass. Danthres had commented at one point that they were going to need to make New Barlin bigger.

As they entered the squadroom—empty save for Sergeant Jonas, as the other four detectives were still out on their cases—Danthres finished her story. "Sorlin didn't really have set family units. Everyone took care of everyone else. I lived with Javian's parents, but pretty much all the adults took care of all the children. But we never had that many infants—most of the children of Sorlin were refugees, but they usually came older."

"Didn't any of the people there have children of their own?"

Danthres shrugged out of her cloak and hung it on the pegboard. "It went in waves. We'd have no pregnancies for years, and then several at once. Rodolfo arrived during one of the fallow periods, so everyone wanted their turn taking care of him." She smiled wryly. "It was kind of disgusting and rather adorable at the same time."

As he sat at his desk, Torin regarded her with what Danthres knew to be a quizzical expression. "I believe that's the first time I've heard you use the word *adorable* in a sentence without sneering."

"To be fair, Rodolfo was a very sweet baby."

"When did you learn of his parentage?"

Danthres smirked. "Did you get a good look at him? He has the same eyes and jawline as the Captain. It was obvious."

"Perhaps when the Pirate Queen was alive."

Conceding the point, Danthres said, "Well, it was obvious to me, at least. Tharri and Lil never saw it, but I was always the more observant."

"A quality one hopes for in a detective," Torin said wryly.

"Plus, her story about being in hiding for ten months never made much sense. She was *always* on the bad side of governments and leaders and tyrants, so going away for so long was wildly out of character."

"Unless she was hiding a pregnancy," Torin said, pointing a finger.

"Exactly. A pirate fleet is no place for an infant, plus I'm certain that Kerestha was the father—Rodolfo has his ears and cheekbones. Rodolfo was probably a regular reminder of the lover she'd lost."

"But the question is, did he eventually learn the truth?"

"While I was at Sorlin? No. But I left almost two decades ago, and he's spent the last few years serving *with* the Captain."

"Which is a concern." Torin rubbed his chin, and Danthres had to look away.

When Danthres and Torin had first met, the latter was in the process of growing his thick beard. She had been trying to remember those days, when his cheeks looked like a ravaged forest, by way of dealing with the thin goatee that was all that covered his chin now, but it was a difficult task.

Torin continued. "I'm assuming that, since you didn't inform me of Rodolfo's parentage until we disembarked, that he gave no indication of being aware of the true identify of his mother?"

"No. He did mention an incident when the Captain, while very drunk, revealed her real name."

Eyes widening, Torin said, "Impressive. There are bards all over Flingaria who would pay their weight in gold pieces for that particular bit of information."

Danthres scowled. "All the more reason to keep it to myself, then."

Chuckling, Torin said, "Fair enough. However, the question remains, did he know? If he did, did he resent being abandoned by his mother like that?"

"His tone seemed affectionate," Danthres said, "but you're right. His entire situation screams motivation to kill someone. We need to look into that, and question him here, away from the rest of the crew."

"Agreed. We should send for him—"

"Tomorrow," said a voice from behind Danthres.

She turned to see Captain Dru exiting his office. Staring at his cheeks, which were covered with bits of blond hair, she asked, "Did you neglect to shave this morning?"

Dru grinned. "Nah, I figured I'd try a beard. I figure *somebody* oughtta have one, since Torin ain't got one no more."

"I seem to recall," Torin said, "that your wife objected to beards."

"She objected to *me* havin' a beard. But that was before she saw Torin lookin' like *that* last week."

Danthres laughed, while Torin frowned. Dru's wife Zan had made a rare visit to the squadroom to surprise the captain on his birthday a week earlier to escort him to an eatery for a special night. It was Zan's first time seeing Torin since he'd shaved, and Zan hadn't actually recognized him at first, which got a laugh out of everyone.

"So after thinkin' about it for a week," Dru said, "Zan told me this mornin' that she's fine with me growin' one."

"As long as your marriage will survive," Torin said.

"Anyhow, shift's almost over, so you two're goin' home. Ain't nothin' in the budget for overtime, so talk to whoever you gotta talk to inna mornin'."

"There's still almost half an hour left in the shift," Danthres said defensively.

"And you're spendin' that time fillin' me in."

Danthres sighed. Torin provided the details of the case thus far.

In the midst of this, Dru had gone into the pantry to get a mug of tea, and was now leaning on Dannee's desk—which used to be his when he was a lieutenant—and said, "I ain't even sure we should be takin' this case. This ain't our jurisdiction, an' I'm pretty sure the Pirate Queen's an enemy of the Lord an' Lady."

"Perhaps," Danthres said, "but they did ask for our help. And someone who would murder so prominent a personage should not be allowed to run around free."

"Yeah." Dru sighed. "Fine, but I don't like it. Try to keep a low profile, at least?"

"Unlikely," Torin said, "with half the dockrats in Mermaid Precinct trying to get a look at the *Rising Jewel*."

"Okay, that explains why I got a message from Mannit wantin' more people." Dru sighed. "Hadn't gotten to it yet 'cause'a the damn paperwork. Wish I'd realized how much there was, I wouldn't'a taken the promotion."

"Look, Dru," Danthres said, "I really don't want to wait until morning. They're all trapped on a boat with a murderer. It's going to be hell for them."

"So what? They're *pirates*, Danthres, an' I ain't gonna try to convince Sir Rommett t'authorize overtime to make them comfy. It can wait until mornin'."

Danthres blew out a long breath. "I still think—"

She was interrupted by the time chimes ringing the top of the hour and also the end of the shift. "Think tomorrow," Dru said. "For now, go home, or do whatever you want until then."

Dru went back into his office. Danthres stared dolefully at her partner. "Thank you *ever* so much for your support."

Torin shook his head. "You have my support when I agree with what you're saying or when I don't care about you're saying. You don't have it when I disagree. I'm with Dru, I see no reason to work extra hours to accommodate the comfort of pirates, all of whom are also suspects. And normally, neither would you."

Danthres opened her mouth to respond, then closed it again. She snarled. "Dammit."

"You know I'm right," Torin said.

She smiled. "That's why I said, 'Dammit.' I should know better than to let my emotions get in the way of the case."

"We could hand it off to someone else who has less personal connection."

Danthres shook her head. "No. I doubt Dru would go for it, and neither would Lisson—especially not after all the trouble he had convincing Chamblin that I should investigate. Besides, my personal connection is why I want this closed, and you know we'll do it better than the Shranlaseth or those two shitbrains."

"Thanks a *lot*, Danthres," came a familiar voice from the entryway.

Danthres turned to see the two shitbrains in question, Manfred and Kellan, entering, looking very piqued. "You two look like you're having a rough time of it. Streak coming to an end?"

"We're gonna close this," Manfred said.

At the same time, Kellan said, "We're never gonna close this."

"See?" Torin said with a chuckle. "Partners don't always support each other."

Manfred pointed accusingly at Kellan. "The streak is real, dammit."

"Streaks end," Kellan said. "And ours is gonna die here."

"That's a shitty attitude, Arn."

"It's a realistic one." Kellan shook his head. "Hundreds of people on the docks every day, and nobody saw anything. Pretty sure about twelve of the people we talked to did see something, but it was someone they know or someone they work with or someone they need work from or whatever." He shrugged. "It's the docks."

Torin asked, "Was Boneen able to cast a peel-back?"

"We didn't even ask," Manfred said. "Between you guys and the thing at the Seagull, we figured we were the bottom of the priority list for him."

"Besides, Sir Louff's yacht is right in the middle of the docks. No way we'd be able to clear away everyone so he could cast it."

Manfred shuddered. "'Specially the yacht itself. Sir Louff always got a full crew on board. They switch shifts, an' I tried to get 'im to let us have the thing between shifts, but he wouldn't do it."

"Doesn't he understand what the peel-back does?" Torin asked.

"Yeah, but he don't like magick."

Danthres blinked. "Amazing. I agree with a noble about something." Getting up from her desk, she moved to the pegboard. "C'mon, Torin, I'll buy you a drink at the Chain."

"I'll have to decline," Torin said, a rare response to the notion of a post-shift drink at the Old Ball and Chain. "Jak and I are having dinner at the Dog and Duck."

"Again? You two should just get a room there."

Torin shrugged as he also rose from his chair. "Seavi, that new cook that Olaf hired, is superb."

"He's from Barlin, yes?"

Nodding, Torin retrieved his cloak. "And quite a find. The only reason Jak and I are able to get seated is because Olaf is still grateful to us after the Brightblade case."

Danthres snorted. The inn had fallen on hard times a year ago, as they'd been closed for renovation over the previous winter, and wound up losing business. But when Gan Brightblade and Olthar lothSirhans—two of the greatest heroes of Flingaria—were murdered by a renegade wizard while staying at the inn, it put the Dog and Duck back on the proverbial map. Because Danthres and Torin had caught that case and eventually closed it, the proprietor, Olaf, considered the pair of them to be perpetual honored customers.

"If you want," Torin said, "you could join us?"

At first, Danthres was going to say yes, if for no other reason than to tease the pair of them when they got affectionate with each other. Instead, she said, "No, I think I need a night of drunken debauchery with my fellow guards. It'll distract me from the case."

"Speaking as a fellow guard," Kellan said, "I'm very much with you on this plan."

Emphatically, Manfred said, "Me, too."

"Enjoy," Torin said. "I'll see you all in the morning."

ELEVEN

Torin saw Jak sitting at a rear table in the packed dining area of the Dog and Duck. He waved to Torin, which caused several locks of his dark hair to flop over his eyes. The sight of that never failed to charm the lieutenant.

As Torin sat down, Jak brushed the hair out of his eyes. "I really should cut my hair."

"If you do, I'll grow the beard back." Torin grinned and then kissed Jak.

Just as they broke the kiss, Prova, one of the barmaids, came by. "Evenin', gents. What can I get ya?"

"He'll have a second ale," Torin said, "and I'll have one as well. And I believe we'll share one of Seavi's casseroles."

Prova winced. "I'm sorry, gents, but we're out of paprika, an' Seavi won't make the casserole without no paprika in it. He's kinda fussy that way."

Jak said, "I wasn't really in the mood for a casserole in any case. What about the beef stew?"

"One for each'a ya?" she asked.

"No, we'll share," Jak said, "like we were gonna the casserole. Seavi makes his portions *way* too big."

Snorting, Prova said, "Yeah, Olaf keeps yellin' at 'im not t'do that, 'cause people keep doin' what you two do an' order one for two, but he keeps doin' it anyhow. Be back with your ales in a tick."

Jak turned to face Torin. "How'd you know I'd already had an ale? There's not even an empty mug on the table."

"I tasted it on your lips when we kissed."

"How'd you know I didn't have the ale elsewhere?"

"Because Seavi also brews his own ale, and the Dog and Duck is the only place that carries it, and it has a very distinctive pumpkin flavor."

Throwing his head back and laughing, Jak said, "Wiate's tongue, I love it when you get all brilliant on me." When his head came back forward, his hair flopped in his face again.

Torin shook his head. "And what, pray tell, is so special about Wiate's tongue?" Jak always used different parts of Wiate's body for his interjections relating to the god.

"Well, I'm told that he was quite nimble with it — able to distinguish any taste from any other taste, and just by placing something in his mouth, he could tell you everything about it."

"No wonder he's a god, then." Torin chuckled and leaned toward him, brushing his hair out of his face for him. "I love it when you get all creative on me."

They kissed again. Torin tasted a bit less of the ale this time.

"So," Jak said after they stopped kissing, "I hear a rumor that you're investigating the death of the Pirate Queen."

"Word travels fast."

"Yes, well, everyone's been talking about the Pirate Queen all day since her boat showed up, and whatever investigation you and the half-elf are up to."

Torin rolled his eyes. "You really can call her by her name."

"No, I can't!" Jak rolled his eyes right back exaggeratedly. "Every time I get it wrong, and I'm sick of it."

"Then refer to her as my partner or as a lieutenant. Why half-elf? Or better yet, just pronounce her name properly."

"I've tried."

"Try again."

Jak sighed. "Fine." He closed his eyes, took a deep breath, and said, "Thrandes. No, Dantiss. *Dammit.* I'll try again: Danthes. Argh!" He pounded a fist on the table.

Torin shook his head and chuckled. "All right, try her last name."

"No, that's worse!" Jak held up his hands as if he was going to be struck. "Just let me call her the half-elf in peace."

With a sigh, Torin said, "Very well."

"And you've done a superlative job of distracting me from talking about the case."

"There's nothing to talk about," Torin said defensively. "The Pirate Queen was poisoned, and we're endeavoring to figure out who did it."

"Can't be that hard, can it?" Jak asked. "I mean, I assume she was killed on that boat of hers—what's it called, the *Rising Sun*?"

"*Rising Jewel*, and yes, but that still is a wide field—there are forty-six people serving on that ship."

Jak blinked. "That many? Wow. How do you need that many people just to sail a boat? I mean, you put up a sail, the wind blows it, what more do you need?"

Torin laughed. "Do you truly think that's all there is to sailing?"

"Oh, and you know so much about it?"

"Well, I've never served on a sailing ship, if that's what you mean, but I have studied seacraft. And as it happens, Danthres and I have talked to all forty-six of the Pirate Queen's crew, and I can tell you exactly how you need so many people. There's the quartermaster, who serves as the first mate of the ship, and then the sailing master, who is in charge of navigation. It isn't simply a matter of putting up a sail, you have to know what direction to travel in."

Grinning, Jak said, "You mean they don't just leave it up to chance?"

"Very droll." Torin smiled indulgently at the sarcastic comment. "There's also a swordmaster, who's in charge of weapons, and three boatswains, who serve as the quartermaster's mates, in essence, supervising their instructions. There's also a carpenter—"

"Oh, well, I could get work on a pirate ship, then."

Torin smiled and continued. " —a healer, a cook, and a rigger, and everyone I just mentioned has at least one mate, sometimes two or three. Plus, there's a cabin girl, four swabbies, and five sailors."

"And one of them killed the Pirate Queen?"

"Unless they have a stowaway, yes."

Jak frowned. "Why would anyone stow away on a pirate ship?"

"Committing murder certainly seems like one possible motive. The Pirate Queen, after all, has many enemies."

"I suppose." Jak reached for something on the table that wasn't there. "We haven't gotten our ales yet."

"Very observant—you'll make a detective yet." Torin looked around, and saw no sign of Prova. "It is very crowded tonight."

The rest of the inn was a wall of noise, as almost every table was filled with customers. However, one voice from a table behind Torin made itself heard.

"Whaddaya mean there's no casserole?"

Turning around, Torin saw Prova standing nervously at a table that contained a dwarf and a human. The human was somewhat large, and was the one yelling.

"Only reason I came down t'this dump t'eat is 'cause the one thing that piece-of-shit *bahrlan* cook can do right is that damn casserole! Rest of th'food's for shit!"

"I'm sorry, sir, p'raps you—"

The human stood up. "Ain't good enough t—"

"For Xinf's sake," the human's dwarf comrade said, "sit your ass down, Choll! We'll just eat something else!"

"That shit-suckin' *bahrlan* don't make nothin' good 'cept that casserole!"

"We didn't come here for the food, we came here for the bard. Sit down!"

Choll sat down and said, "Fine, just get me 'nother ale."

Prova nodded and quickly moved away from the table.

Torin had been ready to interfere in the situation—he was still in his armor of office, after all, as he hadn't had time to go home and change clothes—but the dwarf had calmed Choll down enough that he wasn't needed.

Jak stared at him. "You were going to interfere, weren't you?"

"If necessary."

"You're off duty, Torin. You don't have to get involved when you're not even being paid."

Torin smirked. "If nothing else, I had a certain interest in making sure that Prova didn't get hurt before she brought us our ales."

Chuckling, Jak said, "Fair point."

"I didn't know there'd be a bard this evening."

Jak nodded. "That's why I wanted to come tonight. I also wanted it to be a surprise. Medinn's supposed to be performing."

Torin was taken aback. "Medinn is back in town? I had no idea. He hasn't been back since Lady Meerka's birthday."

"Yes, I heard he was going to be here tonight and then at that festival in Jayka Park next week. I remember you mentioning seeing him back last year."

Nodding, Torin said, "After he performed for Lady Meerka, he did several engagements in taverns throughout the city-state. I saw him at the Stone Kobold." He smiled. "He even told a story of the Pirate

Queen—he said he'd told it to Lady Meerka and she'd enjoyed it tremendously."

Jak pointed to the front of the dining area. "Look, Olaf's getting on the stage."

Following his gesture, Torin saw that the round figure of the Dog and Duck's proprietor was walking onto the raised platform at the front of the dining area where performers plied their trade.

Raising his short arms over his bald head, Olaf said something incomprehensible, but soon the crowd noise died down, as more and more people realized that the evening's entertainment was about to start.

When the crowd noise had dimmed to a low susurrus of murmurs, Olaf said, "Hello to everyone who being here is, thank you!"

Torin hung his head. Olaf was from the islands to the east, but he'd been in Cliff's End for almost two decades. The accent was, Torin knew, a silly affectation, but Olaf did insist on keeping it.

"I must regret to informing you be doing that Medinn will be performing *not* to us this evening that is fine."

The susurrus grew louder and more agitated.

"A caravan he was to be arriving on yesterday from the Iaron place, but not arrive, that caravan has. Sorry I am being, but perform he cannot when here he is not."

Torin nodded, understanding. Caravans to Cliff's End were rarely prompt at the best of times, and it had been far from that since the fire in Barlin. Torin had to admit to being surprised that a professional of Medinn's caliber would even make an engagement in Cliff's End for anything sooner than a week after his scheduled arrival.

"Instead, we are having from Barlin a new performer! Please to be welcoming the harp player, Tarsos Fann!"

There was a smattering of applause, but not as much as Torin would have expected.

"What the shit, Olaf?"

Turning, Torin saw that Choll, the disagreeable human, had stood up again.

"Choll, sit *down*," his dwarven companion was saying, but Choll was having none of it.

"Bad enough we gotta share the damn streets with *bahrlans*, bad enough we gotta eat their food an' watch 'em take our jobs, an' mess up the whole damn city-state, now we gotta listen to their shit-suckin' *music*, too? Hell with that!"

Torin moved to rise, but Jak put a hand on his arm. "Torin, don't, please."

"I'm sorry, Jak, but I cannot let him continue to disrupt things." Shaking off his lover's hand, he came away from the table and approached the human.

Even as he did, he heard several people making noises of agreement with Choll's sentiments.

"Sir, I'm going to have to ask you to sit down and remain silent."

Choll folded his large arms over his barrel-shaped chest. "An' what if I don' wanna?"

The dwarf stood up. "You shitbrain, that's a member of the Castle Guard! Will you *please* sit down?"

"Hell with it." Choll unfolded his arms, drank down the last of his ale, and slammed the mug on the table. "I ain't stayin' in this shithole. Let's go, Maranig."

The dwarf shot an apologetic look to Torin as he tossed a couple of silver pieces onto the table and followed Choll out the door.

While this had been going on, several other people got up and left the dining area, and a short man was setting up a harp on the stage. Torin assumed that to be Tarsos Fann.

As he returned to his table, he saw Olaf approaching.

"Thanking you I am doing, please, Lieutenant. I was worried that fight starting he would be doing."

"Happy to be of help, as always, Olaf."

"As usual," Jak muttered.

Olaf wandered off and Torin sat back down at the table. "What's wrong?" he asked Jak.

"You could've gotten yourself hurt if that toad had decided to get violent. He's twice your size."

"I've handled perps who were twice my size in the past," Torin said with a smile.

But Jak wasn't smiling. "He wasn't a 'perp,' Torin, he was just a person expressing an opinion. And you all but kicked him out!"

"First of all, it was an idiotic opinion. Secondly, he was expressing it by shouting across a crowded dining room, which was very obviously designed to be provocative."

"He was upset," Jak said. "And can you blame him? This place has been a madhouse since all the people from Barlin came in. We only get to eat here because Olaf likes you and the half-elf, otherwise we'd never fit thanks to the damn *bahrlans*."

"Oh, now they're *bahrlans*, are they?" Torin wasn't liking the tenor of this conversation at all.

Prova came by with their two ales, and a grateful smile. "Thanks, Torin, for gettin' ridda that shitbrain. He comes in here every damn night and bitches and moans about the people from Barlin—an' half the time, he tries to reach under my skirt! Anyhow, these two ales're onna house."

She smiled and walked away.

"Oh yes," Torin said, "definitely just a person expressing an opinion."

"He's a piece of filth," Jak replied, "but that doesn't mean he was wrong. Do you know how much harder it's been to get work since they arrived?"

"What happened to that theatrical production you were working on?"

Jak sipped his ale and then let out a belch. "They let me go. Apparently, they're no longer doing *The Fall of Iaron*. I had an entire build set up for that, including several sections of the baron's castle and a re-creation of the mountainside. But instead, they're now doing a play from Barlin called *Hoklo's Revenge*, which has no actual sets, merely two stools. So no carpenters needed, all so they can toady to the—" Jak cut himself off. "Dammit. Look, I'm sorry, Torin, I'm obviously in an abominable mood. I had been counting on that theatre gig."

Torin put his hand on Jak's. "I understand, of course. Look, I'll pay for dinner tonight, and then we can go back to my place for a *proper* apology."

Jak grinned. "I think that's an excellent idea."

The sound of strings rang out through the dining room as Fann started to tune his harp. Again, the room started to quiet down, and Fann started to play.

His third note was very obviously off. So was his fifth. And his tenth.

Torin winced.

"Are you all right?" Jak asked.

"I'm fine." But then another wrong note, and he winced again.

"Is the music that bad?" Jak asked.

Recalling that his lover was tone-deaf, Torin said, "Back home in Myverin, some of my earliest training had been in music and art. You see, I was being groomed to replace my father as Chief Artisan once Grandfather died and my father was elevated to the role of High Magistrate. So I'm afraid I'm painfully aware in minute detail just how horrible this musician is."

Fortunately for him, Jak was oblivious to the wrong notes and bad tuning of the harp. Unfortunately for Fann, Torin was not the only one in the dining hall who was less than impressed.

"Get off'a stage!"

"You're wretched!"

"Like a hobgoblin stranglin' a moose!"

"Go back to Barlin where you belong, shitbrain!"

"Yeah, if you'd stayed in Barlin, your harp woulda burned, and we'd all be better off!"

"Filthy *bahrlan*!"

"Go bang your head against it, it'll sound better!"

By the time the song was over, people were starting to throw their food at Fann.

"Typical *bahrlan*," Jak muttered.

Torin sighed, and watched as Fann left the stage in a hurry, pursued by flung food.

TWELVE

DANTHRES WAS SURPRISED TO SEE THE SQUADROOM COMPLETELY EMPTY AT the beginning of the shift.

Captain Dru and Sergeant Jonas were both in the pantry, eating Jonas's wife's usual offering of morning pastries.

Going inside to partake of her own share of same, Danthres asked, "Where is everyone?"

"Well, your partner's late," Dru said with a grin.

"That's hardly news," Danthres said with a dubious expression right back at him. "And you've got pastry flakes in your beard."

The grin widened. "Yeah, ain't it great? I'm likin' this beard thing." Flicking the offending crumbs out of his nascent facial hair, Dru went on: "Manfred and Kellan worked two straight shifts—they spent the night down at the docks tryin'a catch the graffiti artist. No luck, so I sent 'em home to sleep it off, and they'll come back at it tomorrow mornin'."

Danthres took a perverse pleasure in their having trouble maintaining their idiotic streak, but said nothing, as that pleasure warred with her hating to see a case not get put down, regardless of the circumstances.

"Aleta an' Dannee're down at the Seagull with Boneen. Dannee figured first thing in the morning, the Seagull was pretty likely t'be empty. 'Cept for last night's drunks, anyhow, an' Aleta can take care'a them, no problem."

"Yes, but then we'll have more homicides on our hands," Danthres said dryly as she grabbed a pastry. "Very well. I sent one of the youth squad to Mermaid to request that someone bring us our witness from the *Rising Jewel*."

"Good. We can have a contest to see who gets here first, the witness or Torin."

Danthres chuckled. "He went out with Jak last night, my money would be on Rodolfo."

"That's the Pirate Queen's kid, right?"

Nodding, Danthres said, "And I'm still not entirely sure he knows that. If he does, he becomes our best suspect. If he doesn't, though, it's going to devastate him."

Jonas swallowed a pastry and then asked, "Should I even bother doing the morning rundown?"

Dru grinned. "Just do it in here. I'm still hungry, and it's just us three anyhow."

Shuffling parchments, Jonas said, "Whatever you say, Captain."

Danthres rolled her eyes a bit. Jonas had worked for years under Captain Osric, who had brought a certain relaxed military efficiency to the detective squad. With Dru — after the brief, pathetic reign of Captain Grovis, which had only lasted as long as the equally brief and pathetic reign of Lord Blayk — it was really only the relaxed part. Dru came up through the ranks of the Castle Guard, and unlike Osric, who came straight from being an army general, and certainly unlike his predecessor Brisban, whose death was one of the few Danthres had ever celebrated, Dru had consideration for the workaday guards and lieutenants that neither previous captain had truly had. For that reason, he ran a much more casual squadroom than even Osric had.

While Danthres had no problem with that, indeed rather enjoyed it, a year later, Jonas still hadn't adjusted.

Reading off one parchment, Jonas said, "Dragon Precinct is reporting a disturbance in the Dog and Duck last night. A bard from Barlin was performing and was booed off the stage. Nobody was hurt, but it's the fifth incident at the Dog and Duck involving refugees."

Dru snorted. "I wonder if Olaf thinks that's good or bad for business."

"Torin was there last night," Danthres said. "That was where he and Jak went for dinner. I wonder if he was present for that."

"Maybe we're lucky," Dru said, "an' he's the reason there wasn't a bigger disturbance."

"Hope so."

Jonas shuffled to another parchment. "Manticore Precinct has reported five prisoners trying to jump overboard since word got out that the Pirate Queen's boat is in dock."

"Five?" Dru dropped both his jaw and his pastry. "Shit. That's what we usually get in a *month*, not a day."

"Wait, what? You mean to tell me that every month five shitbrains actually try to escape the barge?" Danthres still had a hard time thinking of the prison barge that sailed the Garamin Sea and housed all of Cliff's End's prisoners as a precinct, even though Lord Doval had transformed it into Manticore Precinct and folded its staff into the Castle Guard.

"On average." Dru shook his head. "I didn't realize it was that many until we started gettin' reports from 'em after they got made part'a the Guard. It's nuts — I mean, it ain't like it's a secret that the bracelets they wear get heavy when you leave the boat."

"Every time I think I've underestimated the populace of this city-state, something reminds me that I generally overestimate it."

"You an' Torin better close this Pirate Queen murder fast. Mannit's crawlin' up my ass 'bout the extra guards to keep the gawkers away."

"Honestly, he can let them run wild," Danthres said. "Boneen has warded the area around the ship, so only members of the Castle Guard can get on or off the boat. For that matter, the boat itself is pretty heavily warded, so I doubt anyone could just get on."

"Nah, 'cause the carpenter's guild is tryin'a join Mannit up my ass. They don't like havin' so many people near the construction zone. Hell, some'a the boardwalks ain't done yet, and they ain't been stress tested yet. Folks could fall in."

"And join the five monthly prisoners at the bottom of the Garamin?" Danthres asked with a smile.

"Yeah." Dru snorted. "Look, we need to get that boat the hell outta here, so hurry up with this."

Danthres shrugged. "Just need my partner and my witness."

A voice came from the squadroom. "Where the hell is everyone?"

Poking her head out the pantry door, Danthres saw Gonzal, Jayson, Rodolfo, and Voran, the Pirate Queen's cook, which was one more person than she expected to see.

"Rodolfo, thank you for coming," she said, exiting into the squadroom. "Voran, why are you here?"

"I have an important matter I must discuss with you and your partner, Lieutenant. It's not something I can share with my shipmates."

Rodolfo looked disdainfully down at the cook. "Which I find impossible to credit."

Holding up both hands, Voran said, "It has nothing to do with *Rising Jewel*. It has to do with my life before I signed up. But it's something I can only talk to them about."

Danthres found this fascinating, especially since Voran hadn't said much of substance in his interview, nor given any indication that he was hiding anything. To Jayson she said, "Put Cook here in three and Rodolfo in one."

Jayson nodded and guided Voran toward interrogation room three on the far end of the squadroom's south wall. Gonzal said, "C'mon," and guided Rodolfo to the door on the nearer end, right next to the pantry.

After doing so, Jayson said, "By the way, Lieutenant, that gnome feller had a message for ya. Said there ain't no stowaway that they found. Same forty-six people been on the ship the whole time."

Danthres nodded, and the two guards from Mermaid Precinct took their leave, passing Torin as he entered.

"Good timing," Danthres said. Then she caught sight of her partner's face. "What's wrong?"

Plastering a smile on, Torin said, "Nothing, just a rough night." He hung his cloak on the pegboard.

"Everything okay with Jak?" Danthres asked.

Torin opened his mouth, closed it, then let out a long exhalation. "May we please talk about it tonight, after the shift ends? It's going to require a rather protracted conversation, and it's one that will require copious amounts of ale."

"Understood," Danthres said. "And agreed, as we don't have time for protracted conversation. Having the *Rising Jewel* in dock is causing all kinds of problems." She filled Torin in on Mannit's complaints, the carpenters guild's complaints, and Manticore Precinct's report.

"Five? Well, I suppose being a pirate is preferable to being a prisoner."

"And two of our pirates are in interrogation. Besides Rodolfo, the cook volunteered to be questioned. Said he had something that could only be spoken of to you and me and relates to his life before signing aboard with the Captain."

"Interesting."

"I doubt it. Probably some matter that relates to why he ran away to join a pirate ship. Let's let him stew in three for a while, I want to get to Rodolfo."

"Agreed — how do you wish to handle the revelation of his parentage?"

"Let's see how it goes. If he knows, we'll proceed as needed, but if he doesn't know, I'd like to be the one to tell him."

Torin nodded. "Very well. Shall we?"

Danthres opened the door to the interrogation room. Rodolfo was leaning on the table rather than sitting in the uncomfortable stool on the other side of it, which was where interview subjects were generally instructed to sit.

"I like this room," Rodolfo said with a smile. "The one lantern, no windows, uncomfortable chairs — it's a clinic in making someone ill at ease."

Torin shot Danthres a look of appreciation, then said, "Please, have a seat in the uncomfortable chair, Boatswain."

Rodolfo smiled. "I'd rather stand, truly."

"Even after walking all the way across the city-state?" Torin asked, sounding surprised.

Shrugging, Rodolfo said, "I am on my feet most of every day. I'm used to it."

"Nonetheless," Danthres said, "we'd like to sit, and we'd rather you sat as well."

"Whatever you say, Thressa."

Danthres winced. It was one thing for Rodolfo to be familiar when it was just the two of them in the *Rising Jewel* wardroom, but in here… "Under the circumstances, I think it would be best if you referred to me by my rank, Boatswain."

Sitting in the stool, Rodolfo contritely said, "Of course, Lieutenant, my apologies."

As she sat in one of the two chairs, Torin doing likewise next to her, Danthres asked, "How much do you remember of your arrival at Sorlin?"

"Bits and pieces. In all honesty, my first memory is waking up in Tharri's arms. Sorry," he added, "I mean in Elsthar Javian's arms."

"I know to whom 'Tharri' refers," Torin said, "as I met the gentleman a year ago. You were only a month old or so when you came to Sorlin, from what Lieutenant Tresyllione has told me. Have you any memories prior to that?"

Rodolfo frowned. "A vague notion of being in a cave with the Captain."

Danthres asked, "Did the Captain ever tell you who your parents were?"

"She didn't know. That wasn't unusual," he added quickly, "most of the halfbreed children she rescued had lost their parents or had been abandoned. Or their parents had already been killed by the purity squads."

Torin folded his hands on the rickety wooden table that was between the detectives the interview subject. "You told Danthres that the Pirate Queen revealed her true name to you."

"Yes, her name was Lillyana."

"That is information that is not easy to come by. I joked with Danthres when she told me that every bard in Flingaria would pay all the gold they had to learn the Pirate Queen's real name."

"I suppose. But she seemed to be speaking to me in confidence." Rodolfo smiled. "Well, truthfully, she told me when she was *very* inebriated. I suspect that, had she been sober, she would never have dreamt of revealing it. I'm not even sure she recalled doing so." He leaned forward and talked in an almost conspiratorial whisper. "Forgive me, Lieutenant, but what does my past and the Captain confiding in me have to do with this investigation?"

Danthres cut Torin's response off. "We ask the questions in this room, Boatswain, and my next one is simply this: why did you sign onto the *Rising Jewel*?"

Rodolfo held his hands palms-up toward the ceiling. "I needed *somewhere* to go when Sorlin was dissolved. I had sailing experience, and the Captain *is* the one who saved my life. Besides—" He hesitated. "I realize I'm not supposed to ask a question, but I need to ask this in order to answer yours: how much do you know about nautical tradition in Flingaria?"

"I'm familiar with the science of seacraft," Torin said, "but I've never actually served on a vessel, so I'm afraid I know only what I've heard from working in Cliff's End this past decade."

"Only the second part for me," Danthres said. "My knowledge of sailing is limited to knowing that wind is involved."

"Ah. That explains it."

"Explains what?" Danthres asked.

"*Letashia* went down in a hurricane. I was one of only a handful of survivors. Generally, those who go down with a ship that is lost at sea are venerated. But if there are only a tiny number of survivors, those people are vilified. They didn't go down with the ship, and if they were able to save themselves, why didn't they save others?"

"That's the most idiotic thing I've ever heard," Danthres said, meaning it. "And I hear many idiotic things on a daily basis, so I do *not* say that lightly."

"It's why I returned to Sorlin after *Letashia* went down. I had no other recourse, at least with a legitimate boat."

"An illegitimate boat, though," Torin said, "was fair game?"

Rodolfo nodded. "The Captain took me and the others aboard with no questions asked. She knew all of us anyhow."

"And she made you boatswain?" Danthres asked.

"Not right away—I was boatswain's mate, but I was promoted relatively quickly, because I knew my way around a boat. And—" He hesitated. "The boatswain to whom I was mate jumped overboard one night a few weeks after I signed on. We never did find out why."

"So," Danthres said, "you never knew why the Captain confided in you with her real name, you never knew your parents, you never knew why she made you boatswain."

"I told you, the boatswain committed suicide, and—"

"And normally," Torin said, "a boatswain's mate wouldn't ascend until being on board for at least a year, prior experience notwithstanding. After all, every boat is different, and it would take that long for you to master all the procedures on board, especially those that differed from those of the *Letashia*. Yet, she favored you."

"I—I suppose." Rodolfo seemed confused.

Danthres decided to go for broke. "So you're unaware who your parents are?"

"You keep asking me that, Thressa!" Rodolfo's voice had raised considerably, and he stood up. "I've been very patiently asking your very invasive questions, most of which have nothing to do with the Captain's murder."

"Sit down, Rodolfo," Danthres said in a very quiet tone.

To Danthres's relief, Rodolfo was properly cowed by her tone and sat quietly.

"Now then," she said, "please answer my question. Are you unaware of who your parents are?"

"I am, in fact, unaware, as you well know, *Lieutenant*, because I believe I was fairly consistently referred to as an orphan during my time in Sorlin. And it didn't matter, because the community of Sorlin raised me, including you. So no, I'm not aware of who my parents are, nor do I give much of a damn, because they don't *matter*. My father provided a pelvic thrust, my mother carried me for nine months, but those are as nothing compared to the lifetime of support I got from the community. And you should *know* that, Thressa!"

An awkward silence followed. Torin sat waiting, she knew, for Danthres to say what obviously needed to be said.

She almost didn't want to say anything, but she had come this far.

"Rodolfo — Lillyana, the Pirate Queen, was your mother."

For several seconds, Rodolfo simply stared at Danthres.

Then he burst out laughing.

"Something amuses you?"

After catching his breath, Rodolfo said, "I believe this should challenge the absurdity of a taboo against sailors who failed to die at sea during a hurricane as the most idiotic thing said in this room today." He laughed some more. "The Captain could not possibly have been my mother."

"And yet," Danthres said, "all the facts support it."

"What facts?"

She started to enumerate points on her fingers. "Fact: before bringing you to Sorlin as an infant, the Captain was in hiding for ten months. She claimed it was to avoid someone out to kill her, but someone was *always* out to kill her. However, it was enough time for her to not be seen while pregnant. Fact: she told you her real name, something she has never shared with anyone else, as far as can be known. Fact: she made you boatswain ahead of schedule. Fact: you have the same eyes as the captain, and the same jawline."

"But — That just — " He shook his head. "Why wouldn't she tell me?"

"Because," Torin said, "being known to have a child would be a vulnerability for her. You'd be a target for anyone who wished to get at her through her offspring."

"Also," Danthres added, "I'm fairly certain that your father was Kerestha. He and the Captain were lovers, and he died after you were conceived but before you were born. You may have been a reminder she didn't wish to have of his death."

Rodolfo looked down at the floor. "I just — I — " He stood up. "This is madness! Why would you tell me this *now*, Thressa?"

Danthres stood up and put her hands on his shoulders. "Because I wasn't sure if you knew. And if you did find out, and find out that she kept this from you, it's a reason to have killed her."

"Killed her?" He shrugged her hands off and backed away from her into the corner of the interrogation room. "You're mad! I loved her as much as I did all of you! Even not knowing she was my mother, I adored her as much as I would have my mother, and as much as I did everyone in Sorlin! I would sooner kill myself than kill her!" Tears started to well up in his black eyes and streak down his prominent cheeks. "And I had no idea she birthed me." Palming away a tear, he added, "Though now that you spell it out..."

"It makes sense. I actually figured it out years ago, but I assumed the Captain had her reasons for keeping it secret."

"Pardon another question, but what happens now?" Rodolfo asked as he collapsed back onto the stool.

Torin rose. "Now you wait here. Danthres?"

Danthres hesitated, and then followed Torin out of the room.

Once she closed the door behind her, she regarded her partner. "I don't think he did it."

"I'm still not convinced he didn't."

Danthres was about to question her partner's skepticism when Dru came out of his office.

"How'd it go?" the captain asked.

"Still not quite sure yet," Torin said. "You wouldn't happen to know about naval traditions, would you?"

Rolling his eyes, Dru said, "More than I ever needed to. Hawk wanted to buy a boat, remember? And he used to go sailing with his grandfather. So yeah, I heard all about every sailing custom in the history of Flingaria. Why?"

"If a sailing ship goes down in, say, a hurricane, and most hands are lost, are the few who survive ostracized?"

"Oh yeah. Hawk told me this story his grandfather told him about a ship called the *Roobin* that got sunk, an' three people survived. They all died poor, 'cause nobody'd hire 'em."

Torin nodded. "All right then, I'm starting to come around to the notion that he didn't do this. However, I'd like to check the nautical records, see if we can verify what he said about the *Letashia*."

"What about the *Letashia*?" came Dannee's voice from the doorway. She was entering the squadroom with Aleta.

"You know of it?" Danthres asked.

Dannee nodded. "My mother was in a performance of *The Wreck of the Letashia.*"

Rolling her eyes, Danthres said, "Of *course* they made a theatrical production of it."

"Do you know anything of the real story of the ship?" Torin asked her.

"Oh yes. Mother always researched every part she did as best she could. The *Letashia* went down in one of the great hurricanes. Only four people survived, and three of them were dwarves. The play is about the three of them."

"What about the fourth?" Torin asked.

"The play doesn't really do anything with him. He was a half-elf."

"I don't suppose you recall his name?"

Dannee winced. "I'm afraid not, Lieutenant, sorry."

Before Torin could say anything else, Dru interrupted. "It's fine—what about the peel-back, Boneen get anything?"

Aleta said, "He got everything, in fact. He's creating a crystal with the image of the perpetrator in his lair right now. Once he provides it, we'll show it to the victim's brother, see if he recognizes him."

"Good." Dru then turned to Torin. "Now then, how'd that *really* go?"

"In light of your verification of naval legend and Dannee's verification of the fate of the *Letashia*, I'm more inclined to believe his story that he didn't kill her—and he definitely didn't know she was his mother."

"You think his surprise was genuine?" Dru asked. "I'm guessin' he at least acted surprised?"

"He did," Torin said, "but it wasn't that that convinced me, it was his complete lack of caring of who his parents were."

Danthres added, "Sorlin is—was a very inclusive community. We didn't have family units, the entire community was *one* family. We all took care of each other."

"Rodolfo never learned who his mother was because it wasn't a fact that interested him," Torin said. "He's sufficiently intelligent that I believe he would understand her motives for keeping his parentage secret, and he was sufficiently cared for by the people of Sorlin that his not knowing wasn't a deception that would have scarred him enough to motivate him to commit homicide."

"So not our guy," Dru said. "What about the cook?"

"I suppose we can talk to him now," Danthres said, "but I can't imagine he'll say anything useful."

"Only one way to find out," Torin said with a grin.

They went into interrogation room three and saw Voran, picking away at one of the splinters on the wooden table. He looked up and seemed relieved to see the two detectives enter. "Finally. I was starting to worry that you forgot about me."

"My apologies, good sir," Torin said, "but we had requested Rodolfo's presence. We had very specific questions for him that required immediate answers. Now that they have been provided, we shall turn our attention to you. I'm Lieutenant Torin ban Wyvald, and I believe you met my partner, Lieutenant Danthres Tresyllione, on the *Rising Jewel*."

"Yes, of course. I'm Voran."

Danthres sat down on one of the chairs, though Torin remained standing. She said, "Yes, the ship's cook."

"I'm afraid I'm much more than that. You see, my work as the ship's cook was a cover for my true purpose on *Rising Jewel*. I'm not actually from Treemark, I'm from Iaron, and I'm part of a group called the Cabal for a Better Flingaria."

Danthres had to admit that this was *not* what she had expected. Though it was kind of the cook to provide himself with a perfect way to make himself an ideal suspect, especially since they'd pretty much eliminated Rodolfo as one.

"Our goal was to convince the Pirate Queen to take her proper place on the Silver Thrones in Velessa."

For the second time in this conversation, Voran said something Danthres did not expect. "I beg your pardon?"

"You see, the Pirate Queen's real name is Lillyana — the older sister to Queen Marta, and the rightful heir to rule the human lands."

THIRTEEN

ALL KUSTRO WANTED TO DO WAS KISS THE BOY.

He'd been working the docks since he grew hair on his nethers. His parents had served as portmasters for two different sections of the docklands, and Kustro did scut work for them both, later becoming a portmaster himself. In fact, he was the youngest person ever to be made a portmaster, but considering that he grew up with it, it wasn't surprising that he knew more about how things ran on the Cliff's End docks than people twice his age.

At least until Lord Blayk took over from Lord Albin. Then, all of a sudden, the portmaster positions were streamlined. Where the docks used to be divided into a dozen sections, Lord Blayk halved that, leaving six portmasters out of work—and three of them were Kustro and his parents. His parents hired on as deputy portmasters under their former colleagues, but Kustro wasn't willing to take a pay cut to do the same job—and have to report to someone who had been his equal a week before.

Then Lord Blayk was arrested for something—Kustro didn't know the specifics, and the rumor mill was on full for that one. Based on what the sailors around the docks were saying, Blayk was arrested for anything from patricide to attempted murder of the king and queen to embezzling tax funds to attempted murder of Lady Meerka. Kustro didn't really care, he was just happy that the person who'd cost him his livelihood and who'd maimed his parents' livelihood was now in a dungeon somewhere or hanged.

Unfortunately, his brother Lord Doval didn't make things any better. He seemed to think that six sections of dock were sufficient, and kept things as they were.

Kustro tried to work as a deckhand, but he quickly discovered something about himself that he'd managed not to learn despite living and working on the docks for a decade and a half: he got seasick.

It was embarrassing more than anything. He'd worked with seafaring vessels his entire life, spent more time near the Garamin Sea than anywhere else, yet it took him until he was almost thirty before he learned that he couldn't go on a seafaring craft without being violently ill.

His parents were kind enough to support him while he tried to figure out what he could do for a living. Even if he was willing to be a deputy portmaster, all those positions were filled, and nobody else would hire him for a lesser position given that he was a qualified portmaster. "The job would be beneath you," they kept saying, even though what was really beneath him was starving to death.

Midwinter was slow, of course, as it always was, and then spring came with first the Gorvangin rampages, and then the influx of refugees from Barlin after the fire.

The former were disastrous, as two of the victims of the rampages were Kustro's parents. The latter meant there was more work at the lower levels that refused to hire Kustro.

But eventually, both those problems worked in his favor. For one thing, he inherited his parents' small house on the River Walk, so he had a place to live. And with so many people pouring into Cliff's End, employers were less fussy about who they would employ, and Kustro found himself doing scut work up and down the docks.

He had applied to fill one of his parents' positions as a portmaster, but they instead promoted two deputy portmasters and hired other people to take over as deputies to replace them. Kustro was more than a little bitter about that.

There was plenty of work, at least, so he could continue to feed and clothe himself. But he wanted to be a portmaster again. With actual seafaring work cut off thanks to his weak stomach, that was where his ambitions lay.

His work ambitions, anyhow.

One of his many gigs was to be one of the deck cleaners for Sir Louff's yacht when it was in dock—which is was regularly, as the nobleman didn't actually like to go out to sea very often. What he liked was being able to say he had a yacht.

It was on that gig that he met Asch.

Asch was Sir Louff's nephew, and he was in charge of the yacht when the nobleman wasn't around — which was a great deal of the time.

It was lust at first sight for Kustro, who found himself doing something he'd never done before: do poorly on a job so he'd be called back to fix it and do it better.

Of course, doing so risked him getting fired, but it meant spending more time near Asch.

For a long time, he said nothing, content to admire Asch from afar.

But then there was the first really hot day of the year, when Asch was out on the deck sunning himself completely naked.

From that moment on, Kustro was determined to, at the very least, kiss Asch.

He volunteered for more shifts on the yacht so he could be near him. If a higher-paying job presented itself that conflicted with time he'd committed to Sir Louff, he prioritized Sir Louff so he could gaze upon Asch's form.

Everything in Kustro's life had gone to shit. He was barely making enough coin to survive, and then only because he inherited his home — and he would gladly have given that up to have his parents back. He had been cut off from his calling, stuck working for the people who should have been his peers.

But he had Asch's beautiful body to stare at. It was crude, it was base, but at least it gave him one thing to care about.

Eventually, Asch started to notice. At first, Kustro was worried that Asch would take offense, but he seemed to be enjoying the attention. He spent more time sunbathing when Kustro was working, and offering him overtime more than once.

In truth, Kustro had no expectations of anything developing between him and Asch. He was a defrocked portmaster working as a deck hand. Asch was the son of a noble.

But Kustro did want to kiss him just once.

He thought he had the opportunity. It was a morning gig cleaning up after a party on the yacht the night before. Some of the partiers were still passed out and drunk in the common area of the yacht, in fact. Kustro and one other deck hand, a dwarf named Chalsarig, cleaned up all the foodstuffs and half-drunk mugs and filthy bits of furniture.

Asch asked Kustro to come up to the bridge, and Kustro did so.

"Do you find me attractive, Kustro?"

Kustro found himself unable to speak.

"No need to answer," Asch said. His voice was like honey, as beautiful as the rest of him. "I know you do by the way you stare at me. Tell me, do you have any plans to further this attraction?"

"I would never presume," Kustro stammered.

"You may presume."

"I—I simply wish to—to kiss you."

Asch blinked in surprise. "Is that all?"

"Yes."

"Interesting. I believe that I can accommodate that request." Asch leaned in, his lips parting.

For the first time in almost a year, Kustro felt happy. He was finally getting something he wanted. Ever since Lord Albin died, everything he'd received had either been something he merely needed or, more likely, something horrible. To actually receive a true gift from the universe seemed a blessing from on high.

"What in Ghandurha's name are you doing?"

Naturally, the gods saw fit to yank that happiness away from him just like everything else. That voice belonged to Sir Louff, who entered the bridge just as Asch was leaning in to kiss him.

Sir Louff was apoplectic at the sight of his son about to kiss him. "How dare you? Bad enough you consort outside the wedding bed, but you do so with another man, and a common deck hand, at that? You," he said to Kustro, "get off my yacht! Don't ever let me see you again!"

Kustro had expected this the moment Sir Louff had invoked Ghandurha. Worshippers of that particular god tended to frown on any form of affection that was outside a marriage contract, and that god also would never bless such a contract (or any manner of contact) between members of the same sex.

Asch did, to his credit, try to stop him. "Father, you shouldn't let Kustro here go. *He* is the one who figured out how to get that Emmegan paint off the prow."

For a brief moment, Kustro thought his job at least might be saved. Sir Louff had been furious about the Emmegan paint, but Kustro knew someone who could get his hands on the only thing that would remove the magickally enhanced paint from a surface. And Kustro right there swore that he would never reveal that source to anyone who worked for Sir Louff if he lost his job.

Unfortunately, that wasn't enough. "I don't care," Sir Louff said, "if he cleaned the entire yacht with his tongue! I will not have *anyone* tempting you away from Zaroa!"

Kustro had no idea who Zaroa was at the time. Later, he found out from Chalsarig that she was the daughter of another noble, and the person to whom Asch was affianced.

And that was that. Kustro wouldn't get to kiss Asch, nor would he keep his best regular source of income.

At first, he was tempted to blow off his afternoon job, which was to prepare a ship for scuttling. It was damaged in a fire, and Kustro was one of the people hired to make a final run through it to make sure everything of value was removed, and often you got to keep anything you did find, above and beyond the silver you were paid.

Kustro decided to go to that job. Partly, he went because it kept him from thinking about the fact that he was likely never again to either see Asch, or ever work for Sir Louff. And partly because he couldn't really afford to alienate *another* employer.

This turned out to be the best thing possible, because when he dug around the cargo hold of the ship, he found a loose deckboard.

Prying the plank completely away, he found a single scroll, which had a seal decorated with the symbol of the Brotherhood of Wizards.

A spell!

Barely, Kustro managed to rein in his excitement. He hid the scroll in his tunic, not willing to take the chance that the boat's owners would simply claim it and just pay him the one silver. Spell scrolls were worth a pretty coin.

Best of all, when he got home that night, he found a package left for him, with a note from Asch. "Consider this severance pay and an apology." Inside the package were five gold coins. A pittance to such as Asch, but it probably salved his conscience. Besides, that was a month's wages for Kustro, so he could hardly complain.

Then he read over the spell on the scroll. It gave the caster invisibility for one hour, and was good for four castings!

He immediately enacted a plan. First, he got some Emmegan paint. Then he cast the spell and painted graffiti on some random boat while invisible. The next night, he did the same to another boat, then to a boardwalk.

For the fourth and final casting of the spell, he did the same on Sir Louff's yacht, right on the hull where everyone could see it.

All four times, he painted the words, "Ghandurha is a louse!"

From what he'd heard, Sir Louff was even more apoplectic than he had been when he'd walked in on Kustro and Asch. Especially since nobody seemed to know how to get the paint off. According to Chalsarig, Sir Louff was even more furious when he found out that the only person in his employ who knew how to get rid of the paint was the one he fired for trying to kiss his son. At which point, he got even angrier, but refused to even consider asking Kustro for help.

Kustro's only disappointment was that he didn't get to watch his meltdown.

That, and that Sir Louff didn't actually die from his head exploding with fury.

Chalsarig also mentioned that the Cloaks were looking into the graffiti, which Kustro didn't really care about. After all, nobody could see him!

He cared a bit more when two Cloaks knocked on his door.

For a brief moment, he considered pretending not to be home, but no. The Cloaks wouldn't just give up, they'd come back again. Best to seem completely cooperative. Besides, the scroll had completely disintegrated after the final use, so there was no evidence that he used it, and he'd sold the remaining paint to a boatswain whose captain was looking for some to touch up the coloring on his figurehead. That vessel had set sail for the south the previous morning.

He opened the door to see two human males, one dark-skinned with very little hair, one light-skinned with a mop of blond hair, both wearing Castle Guard armor with the gryphon medallion on their chests and the brown cloak indicating that they were detectives.

"Are you Kustro Marzi?" the dark-skinned one asked.

Kustro nodded.

"I'm Lieutenant Manfred, this is my partner, Lieutenant Arn Kellan. We have a few questions about Sir Louff's yacht."

"What about it?"

"We understand that you were recently fired from that yacht's cleaning detail."

"Yeah." Kustro decided to be completely honest about this part. "Sir Louff didn't like the way I was looking at his son." He shrugged. "Ghandurha worshipper."

"We got that, yeah," Manfred said with a chuckle. "According to Sir Louff, you were the one who was able to get Emmagen paint off his prow a month ago."

"That's right. I've got a friend who has a line on Jiro ointment—that's the only thing that gets it out, but it's rare as hell."

Manfred nodded. "We're investigating someone who painted 'Ghandurha is a louse!' on several places on the docks, including Sir Louff's yacht."

"I heard about that," Kustro said. "You think it was *me*?"

Kellan finally spoke. "We think it was someone who has a grudge against Sir Louff."

"I worked for Sir Louff for half a year, that's a long list." Kustro grinned.

"And you're on it." Kellan wasn't grinning.

"Well, sure, but I—"

Manfred interrupted. "We need to search your dwelling, Mr. Marzi."

Kustro shrugged, trying to be as casual as he could be. "I guess, if you want to, sure."

He let the two Cloaks in. They checked the entire space, and the closet. Kustro didn't have that much—he'd never had many possessions, and he'd sold what few he'd had over the years.

"All right," Manfred said, "thank you. Hey, has anybody asked your friend for Jiro ointment?"

"Not that I know of, but I haven't spoken to him in over a month."

"Okay. We may be back with more questions. Let's go, Arn."

The two Cloaks departed. As soon as he closed the door on them, Kustro put his ear to the door to try to overhear what they were talking about.

"Dead end number thirteen," he could hear Manfred say.

"If the damn peel-back had given us *something*, but without it, we're never gonna find anything."

"We've still got to talk to Evero. The streak isn't dead yet."

"Yeah, but…"

The rest of Kellan's sentence was inaudible, and Kustro couldn't hear anything else.

He grinned. Evero was a malcontent, but also dirty as hell, even by Mermaid Precinct's high standards. Those two Cloaks would be digging into him for days.

Kustro smiled. He was pretty sure he was home free. He made Sir Louff's life miserable, he'd gotten a month's pay for no work, and it looked like he was going to get away with it.

All he'd wanted was to kiss the boy. He didn't get to do that, but at least he got his revenge.

FOURTEEN

"SAY THAT AGAIN," DANTHRES SAID TO VORAN, "SLOWLY."

"The Pirate Queen's real name is Lillyana, sister of Queen Marta. More to the point, she's her *older* sister. She is the rightful ruler of the human lands, and someone has killed her in order to stymie our efforts to put her on the Silver Thrones where she belongs."

Torin stared at the ship's cook for several seconds, then sat down next to Danthres. "Let's start from the beginning, shall we? You said you're part of a cabal?"

Voran nodded. "Of course. The Cabal for a Better Flingaria. I'm actually a part of a noble family back home in Iaron, but I was sent along to *Rising Jewel* because I can cook."

"That makes you unusual among noble folk I've know," Torin said.

"Here in Cliff's End, perhaps, but in Iaron we value actual skill, not just the ability to hire somebody to do things for you. My parents made sure I had basic survival skills in case something happened, and we found ourselves destitute."

"Very forward-thinking of them," Danthres said.

"Backward-thinking, really." Voran smiled sheepishly. "We lived through the crash. In fact, the crash is pretty much what got the Cabal started."

"The crash was almost ten years ago," Danthres said. "We've recovered."

"*Cliff's End* has recovered because you're the busiest port in Flingaria, and because Lady Meerka was able to start several reinvestment and infrastructure programs that got the city-state back on its feet. And Velessa recovered because the king and queen put their own personal fortunes into the economic recovery, a consideration they didn't bother with for any other locale under their rule. Iaron, Barlin, and Treemark were left to suffer on our own. It took years to recover, and then we had that avalanche in Iaron and then fire in Barlin..." Voran sighed.

Torin rubbed his chin—an action that still felt strange with so little hair there now. He'd had no idea that the other human city-states had suffered worse burdens following the crash than Cliff's End had.

"That action in particular made it clear that King Marcus and Queen Marta only care about Velessa. They take our taxes but do nothing to improve our lives. Here in Cliff's End, you've been able to take matters into your own hands, but the other human lands are less fortunate. So we gathered—there are about two dozen of us, nobles from Iaron, Barlin, Treemark, Velessa, and here in Cliff's End. We are bound and determined to put someone on the Silver Thrones who will be a ruler for *all* humans, not just the ones who live in Velessa."

"This is all *very* fascinating," Danthres said in a tone that made it clear that she truly felt the opposite, "but what does this have to do with why you were on the *Rising Jewel* pretending to be a cook?"

"Well, I *am* a cook, as I said—but," he added quickly, no doubt noticing the look on Danthres's face, "that's not what's important. You see, one of the Cabal members is Sir Urchan, and he's in charge of genealogical affairs for the city-state."

Torin frowned. "Genealogical affairs?"

Voran nodded. "Of course. Isn't there such a person here?"

"Not that I'm aware of."

"Questions of lineage and heredity are important—such things need to be verified in cases of inheritance of lands and titles."

"Ah," Torin said. "Lady Meerka handles such questions. She's in charge of financial matters."

"It's not always financial, but I suppose it often comes down to that." Voran sighed. "In any event, Sir Urchan was digging through some of the older royal records, and he came across a medical report from a healer that King Tomsim's two daughters were both in perfect health. This surprised him, as he thought that Queen Marta was the only child of King Tomsim and Queen Grazia. He investigated further, and discovered that there was an older sister named Lillyana. He even came across a portrait of Marta and her sister, and Lillyana looked *exactly* like the Pirate Queen. By all the laws of the land, *she* would be the one to inherit the throne, but there's no record of her after King Tomsim's death forty years ago—and very few records before that."

"So you were sent to become her cook?" Torin asked. This revelation was one that fascinated the part of Torin that had been trained as a historian back in Myverin, and he was tempted to ask more questions about Sir Urchan's investigations. If nothing else, the timeline matched, as Tomsim's death was indeed forty years earlier, and the Pirate Queen started making a reputation for herself about thirty to thirty-five years previous. But it was the Pirate Queen's death that mattered here, and so he needed to keep the interrogation on track.

Voran nodded. "The records Sir Urchan was able to find indicated only that she existed, up to a point. We had no idea why she wasn't made queen, but given that she turned to a life of piracy, we assumed there to be some scandal, and that she became a pirate to enact revenge on her family. And so I travelled south to Treemark and was able to join her crew. In truth, I had only expected to be a deckhand or the cook's mate, but both the cook and cook's mate had recently departed, and there was an opening. I made a day's worth of meals for the crew and was hired."

"When did you approach the Pirate Queen with your notion?" Torin asked.

"I waited a bit. I wanted to get a feel for what she was like. One thing I noticed was that she seemed to be — well, weary. She'd been at sea for the better part of four decades, after all, and while she looked more youthful than her years, she wasn't *getting* any younger, either. I thought it would be a good time to let her know that there were those who would restore her to her rightful place."

"And how did she respond?" Danthres asked.

"Laughter, at first. She said she wasn't interested, but I kept bringing it up with her, and we had a very long conversation one night over a bottle of wine on the subject. She finally agreed to come back to Velessa with me to claim the Silver Throne."

There was a long pause, and Torin saw that Voran looked a bit stricken.

Finally, he said, "The next morning, she turned up dead in her bunk. I can only assume that she told Chamblin or Lisson or one of the other crew about it — or someone overheard our conversation."

"So you think one of the crew did it?" Torin knew that was an obvious question with an obvious answer, but he wanted to gauge Voran's reaction to it.

"Who else? After all, life under Lillyana was very lucrative. Even my own cut of our profits was not inconsiderable, and I've led a well-off life. To have that taken away could drive one to murder, I would think."

"Quite possibly." Torin looked over at Danthres, who had a faraway look in her eyes. He turned back to Voran. "What was the plan for her taking over?"

"I'm sorry?"

"You said she agreed to your plan. What was the next step?"

"We were going to set sail for Treemark, initially. The Cabal members from that city-state would have taken her in, and eventually we would all converge on Velessa. The plan has been in place for over a year now, but it would take some doing to implement it. Lillyana had said that she would take care of things on the *Rising Jewel*, though I'm afraid she wasn't specific as to how that would happen. I want to emphasize that I'm coming to you with this voluntarily. I know that I've admitted to being part of a conspiracy to unseat the king and queen, and I know that might have consequences, but I feel strongly about the Cabal's cause, and I would rather it be known that I am involved with that than to have committed murder. After all, who better to poison the Captain's food than the cook? Besides, Lillyana is—was—the key to our campaign. With her dead, our hopes and dreams have been dashed." He sighed. "Besides, now that I'm off the boat, I will need to get a message to the Cabal members here in Cliff's End."

"And who might they be?" Danthres asked.

Voran smiled ruefully. "Nice try, Lieutenant, but I'm not about to allow my comrades to be arrested. You have no authority over Sir Urchan, and I'm willing to accept the consequences to myself by admitting to being part of the Cabal, but I will not put any of the Cliff's End members in jeopardy."

Torin got to his feet. "Very noble of you. If you'll excuse us a moment, please."

Danthres also rose, though she seemed briefly surprised by his ending the interrogation. However, she covered it quickly, and Torin doubted that someone who didn't know Danthres as well as he did would have even noticed the change in her facial expression, it was so brief.

They came out into the squadroom, where Aleta and Dannee were going over some scrolls. Torin figured that Aleta was continuing to educate Dannee on the vicissitudes of Castle Guard paperwork. He recalled his own indoctrination in same, and also hoped that Aleta was more patient with Dannee than Danthres had been with him eleven years ago.

As he closed the interrogation room door behind them, Torin said, "We need to verify Voran's account."

Danthres nodded. "That's something I'm sure he is *not* expecting."

Dru came out of his office. "What isn't he expecting?"

Torin and Danthres filled their captain in on the interrogation. While they did so, a guard showed up and handed Aleta a crystal, and she and Dannee went off to find their perpetrator.

"Shit." Dru's eyes had gone wide as saucers upon learning of Voran's claims. "How the hell is the Pirate Queen the heir to the throne?"

"We don't know that she is," Danthres said, holding up a hand. "All we know right now is that her cook—who *claims* to be a noble from Iaron rather than a cook from Treemark—says that she is."

"How the hell does a noble even *learn* to cook?" Dru asked.

Danthres snorted. "He says that his parents insisted that he learn useful skills beyond counting his gold coins."

"A reaction," Torin added, "to the crash a decade ago, which is also what led to this Cabal forming."

Dru shook his head. "Yeah, okay, but still, this sounds nuts."

"Which," Torin said, "is why we need to verify his account. We must go to Velessa and request an audience with the king and queen."

"No way," Dru said. "It's two weeks to Velessa and back. I need this case put down in the next two *days*, not more'n a month from now. That ship can't stay inna docks much longer, or Mannit's gonna quit in disgust. Bad enough with the overcrowding, an' that pirate boat's just makin' it worse. 'Sides, what makes you think the king an' queen'd even *see* you two?"

"Oh, that part's easy," Danthres said. "Remember, we broke Lord Blayk's conspiracy to have them killed. On the final day of the trial last year, both King Marcus and Queen Marta said that they were forever in our debt, and that they would never forget what we did for them." She smiled. "Now frankly, I'm sure they were talking out of their asses, but I'm willing to make a nuisance of myself in the palace until such a time as they see the people who, in essence, saved their lives, since if we hadn't stopped Blayk, he would have taken another shot at killing them — or, at the very least, declared war on the rest of the human lands."

Torin snapped his fingers. "That it!"

"What's it?" Dru asked.

"We don't need a month, we'll only need a day, possibly two. We can get to Velessa the same way we did during the trial."

Danthres snarled. "No."

Dru said, "Boneen teleporting you? Yeah, that'd work."

"I will not go through that twice," Danthres said, hand moving to her stomach.

"Fine," Dru said, "then Torin can go by himself."

Here it comes, Torin thought even as Danthres whirled on Dru. "Absolutely not! He'll botch the whole thing!"

Dru regarded her with a bit of scorn, a look he never would have dreamed of trying on her when they were both lieutenants, but Torin had noted that Dru had more and more grown accustomed to the authority that came with his promotion. "Pretty sure Torin'd be able t'handle it. But if you think it's such a big deal, then suck it up and teleport with him."

Danthres hesitated. "I — "

"Look, goin' on foot ain't an option. We gotta close this fast. Couple more days, an' I want that boat outta here whether or not you found the murderer."

"What about this Cabal?" Torin asked. "We cannot simply ignore it."

Dru shrugged. "Fine, keep the cook around — we can arrest him on conspiracy or somethin' — but the docks're crazy enough between what happened in the Seagull an' the *Rising Jewel* sucking all the air outta the place."

Letting out a very long sigh, Danthres said, "Very well, I'll teleport with Torin."

"Good." Torin nodded emphatically.

Danthres grinned. "Oh, so you agree that you'll botch it without me?"

"No, but your point before about needing to very loudly remind the monarchs of the debt they said they owe us is well taken. I suspect it will be far easier to convince them of their need to grant us an audience if you're there to remind them of that debt in your own inimitable style."

"So you're saying I'm better at being a pain in the ass than you are?" Danthres was still grinning.

Dru rolled his eyes. "We *all* know that."

"Indeed." Torin chuckled.

"All right," Danthres said, "let's go convince Boneen to take us on a trip."

"Not just Boneen," Dru said. "You're gonna need to get an authorization from either the lord or the lady — maybe both."

Danthres said, "I believe I can get that authorization from Lady Meerka." Smiling, she added, "She likes me."

"I'll speak with Boneen," Torin said.

"All right." Dru nodded. "Let's get this done."

FIFTEEN

ALETA WAS EXTREMELY UPSET TO REALIZE THAT THE VISAGE SHE SAW IN Boneen's crystal was one neither she nor Dannee recognized.

"I don't see the problem," Dannee said as they walked down Meerka Way. They were headed to the Lambit residence to see if Ditha recognized the person in the crystal. "I mean, if it wasn't anyone we interviewed, that's good—it means that everyone we talked to told the truth!"

Aleta sighed. "No, that's not what it means. It just means that none of them did it. I'm quite sure several of them saw what happened, but said they didn't so they wouldn't have to testify before the magistrate. And besides, it's much better if you can catch a witness in a provable lie because it gives you leverage to get the truth out of them. If the murderer was one of the witnesses we already talked to, it would be easy to get a confession."

Dannee frowned. "Do we even need one? We have the peel-back."

"Not really. I mean, it helps, but the magistrate prefers additional evidence beyond the peel-back since it's just Boneen's word as to what it shows."

This seemed to shock Dannee. "You mean he doesn't trust a wizard's word?"

"The magistrate doesn't trust *anyone's* word."

They crossed Oak Way into Dragon Precinct, and immediately the streets got more crowded. It was harder for the pair of them to walk two abreast, but Aleta glowered at people who considered obstructing them, and they generally stepped aside.

Aleta continued: "Also if we didn't interview him, it means he had the wherewithal to get out of the pub before the guards showed up, which means he's cautious. It's a lot easier to catch a killer who's overconfident. Ones who are wary and who think things through are more difficult."

"I suppose."

They got to the building that included the rooms rented by the Lambit brothers. The box-shaped building had doors on all four sides, and Aleta went to the one with a numeral four on it, which was around the back.

tenants. Did you find who killed my brother?"

"Not yet," Aleta said, pulling the crystal from the pouch on her belt. "But now we know what he looks like." She held the crystal in both hands, concentrated, and the image of a human male appeared over it. "Do you recognize him?"

"Yes—but I'm afraid I don't know who he is."

"What does that mean, exactly?" Dannee asked.

"I mean, I've seen him before."

"At the Seagull?" Aleta asked.

Ditha shook his head. "No, on the *Dekird*. I saw him talking to our boss, and later he was talking to Soza, but when I asked Soza who he was and what he wanted, he just said it was some guy from the boat, and he didn't say anything else."

"I see." Aleta sighed. It obviously wasn't anyone from the *Dekird* crew because they set sail two days ago—Aleta and Dannee verified that before coming back to the castle—and so the murderer couldn't have been crew.

Or, at least, not crew anymore. "Do you know if he was a sailor on the *Dekird*, or just another cargo hauler like you?"

"Cargo hauler, I think. I mean, I'm pretty sure I saw him carrying boxes."

"Who hired you for that job?"

"There's a broker on the docks, name of Palnitt. Still waiting for him to pay us, honestly."

"I see. Thank you, Mr. Lambit. We'll let you know if we find the perpetrator."

Ditha nodded and closed the door.

Dannee sighed after the door shut. "I don't know this Palnitt person."

Aleta smiled. "Oh, I do."

"Is he reputable?"

"As reputable as anyone on the docks." Aleta held up her hands, palms-up. "Which means, not reputable in the least. But he also is someone I can have a conversation with."

Staring at her quizzically, Dannee asked, "I don't understand. Can't you have a conversation with anyone? I mean, the whole point of the Castle Guard is that we can talk to anyone, especially when a crime's involved."

"That's—that's not quite what I mean. C'mon."

Aleta led Dannee through the crowded thoroughfares to the River Walk, specifically to a white shack at the corner of the River Walk and Darnay's Pass.

As they approached, Aleta rolled her eyes as she sighted a troll standing in front of the door to the shack, huge arms folded over huger chest. In truth, she smelled the troll long before she saw him, which was not surprising, as hygiene wasn't something trolls ever really considered.

"Is that a troll?" Dannee asked.

"Apparently." She approached the troll, looking up at his scowling face, accentuated by the two tusks that jutted upward out of his mouth toward his cheeks. He stood half a head taller than Aleta, who carried the great height typical of elves, but this creature still towered over her. "I need to see Palnitt."

"Palnitt not see no one," the troll rumbled.

"We're lieutenants in the Cliff's End Castle Guard, and we'll see whoever we want. Step aside, please."

"Palnitt not see no one," the troll said again.

Aleta sighed. It had been a while since she'd had to subdue a troll, and she wasn't particularly looking forward to it.

Then Dannee said, "*Effga tenk so vin kel.*"

Shooting her a look, Aleta asked, "You speak troll?"

"The language is called Hargit, and I don't speak it very well, I'm afraid."

The troll said something in the same tongue that Aleta couldn't make out, though it sounded like a lot of harsh syllables thrown together.

"What did he say?" Aleta asked.

Dannee looked resigned. "He basically said 'Palnitt not see no one,' only he said it in Hargit this time."

"Explain to him that we're Castle Guard."

"Okay." Dannee cleared her throat, and then said, "*Asgo so tenk el hak ma rak.*"

The troll responded the same way.

Resigned to the next course of action, Aleta turned and took five steps away from the shack, turned around, and took a deep breath. She was going to need a running start for this.

Dannee just stared at her, confused.

She broke toward the troll, running as fast as her boots and cloak would allow. Briefly, she lamented the Castle Guard uniform that required those, as they hampered movement, though she took solace from the fact that this job required far less physicality than her role as a Shranlaseth agent.

The troll looked first befuddled, unfolding his arms, then surprised as Aleta leapt into the air.

Pulling back her right arm, she struck the troll in the side of the throat with the tips of her fingers.

Bouncing off the troll's massive form, Aleta landed in front of the creature into a crouching position.

For his part, the troll's eyes rolled back in his head, and he fell to the ground in a heap.

Several people had gathered 'round to watch this tableau, which Aleta hadn't given much mind until now, when they broke into applause.

"That was amazing!"

"Troll smells like shit anyhow!"

"How'd she *do* that?"

"Go home, Cloaks, we don't want you here!"

"That'll teach Palnitt t'be an ass!"

"Shit, Palnitt already knows how to be an ass…"

Just another day in Mermaid, Aleta thought with a resigned sigh. She stepped over the troll's prone form and opened the door. Dannee followed a bit more slowly.

Inside the shack was a small desk piled high with scrolls, and two windows that looked out onto the docks. Standing in front of the desk with his arms folded in much the same position as the troll was Palnitt, a thin, elderly human who was far less menacing.

In a reedy voice, he said, "The hell y'be doin' *that* f'r?"

"Your troll wouldn't let us in," Aleta said.

Dannee added, "We even asked him nicely in his own language."

"Doubt that," Palnitt said with a *tch* sound. "Ain't no way t'ask nothin' nicely in Hargit."

"Perhaps," Dannee said, "but we did ask in both Common and Hargit, and he wouldn't let us pass."

"Ain't s'posed to! S'a whole point'a havin' a bodyguard, ain't it?"

Aleta put her hands on her hips. "We've been through this, Palnitt. I sent your first bodyguard who wouldn't let me in to the healer's. The troll, at least, will be okay — I hit a nerve cluster, and he'll wake up in an hour or so with just a mild headache. But your last few bodyguards knew better. Why doesn't this one? And what happened to the last ones, anyhow?"

"Ol' Mags Barstow wouldn't let her boys work f'me no more. Said she found a better-payin' job f'r 'em."

Aleta nodded. Barstow had several children, all of whom were almost as big as the troll outside. They were often hired as muscle, particularly in Goblin, so Aleta wasn't surprised that they got a better offer.

"I figgered a troll'd be perfect. Don't gotta pay 'em as much, anyhow."

"And yet you forgot to tell him to always let the Castle Guard in."

"Yeah, well, trolls ain't known f'r nuance, y'know? I told 'im not to let nobody in, an' that does the trick, most days."

"This day isn't most. I need to know if you've hired this person." She took out the crystal and concentrated.

"Why should I tell you if —"

Aleta rolled her eyes. "Really, Palnitt? I just took out your troll in half a second. Do we *have* to go to the trouble of arresting you?"

"On what charge? I'm legit!"

"Public endangerment having that smelly thing standing outside your shack threatening people."

Palnitt sneered. "It'd never hold up."

"Of course it won't, but you'll still be tied up in the castle for the rest of the day, and maybe all day tomorrow, too. Is it really worth —"

Unfolding his arms, he held both hands out, making as if to push Aleta away. "All right, fine! Y'madejer point." He shook his head. "Damn Shranlaseth. Like dealin' with Manfred an' Kellan more. They're civilized folk."

"They don't pay me to be civilized," Aleta said. "Now, then, who is this?"

Palnitt sighed. "Name's Xeros. Lives inna boarding house onna River Walk. Th'one with'a big fish onna door."

Aleta nodded. "I know the place. Can you tell me anything about him?"

"He hauls cargo. I pay him." Palnitt folded his arms again and stared at Aleta, almost daring her to ask more.

But Aleta didn't take the bait, mostly because she was fairly certain Palnitt didn't actually know anything more about Xeros than that. "Thank you for your assistance."

As she turned to leave, Dannee following, Palnitt yelled to them, "What'm I supposed t'do 'bout that heap'a troll you left on m'doorstep?"

Dannee called back, "I'd suggest some tea when he wakes up—you know, for the headache?"

Unable to help herself, Aleta chuckled.

SIXTEEN

DANTHRES CLUTCHED HER STOMACH AS IT DISGORGED ITS CONTENTS ONTO THE marble floor of Tomsim Castle in Velessa.

"What do you think you're doing?" came a voice from behind her.

Ignoring it, Danthres continued to heave while kneeling on the marble. She had deliberately eaten very little, but sadly her stomach decided to simply dry-heave after being teleported from Cliff's End to Velessa.

Torin's voice sounded soothingly from behind her. "My apologies, sir, but Lieutenant Tresyllione reacts rather poorly to Teleport Spells."

"What *possible* reason would you have to use such a spell to come *here*?" said the first voice. Were Danthres capable of speech, she would have commented on the abject stupidity of asking that question of someone dressed in the armor and cloaks they were wearing.

"We're here," Torin said, "on official business of the Cliff's End Castle Guard." Danthres heard the rustling of paper. "Here is a letter from Lady Meerka authorizing our presence here."

Finally, Danthres's stomach stopped doing backflips, and she clambered to her feet.

Looking around, she saw that she was in the same receiving room of Tomsim Castle that she'd been sent to by Boneen a year ago during each day of the trial of Lord Blayk and his co-conspirators in their plot to kill the king and queen. The massive space had ceilings so high a troll could stand on a troll's shoulders and still have to jump to touch it. At the center of the room was a huge fountain, decorated with hideous statues of wolves and covered in even more ivy than it had had a year earlier. A huge winding staircase led to the upper levels — including, Danthres recalled, the conference room where Blayk's trial was held, as well as the throne room.

A short functionary in a silk shirt, tights, and leather boots was looking over the scroll that Lady Meerka had written on their behalf at Danthres's request. The lady of the demesne had been very generous with her signature and seal once Danthres explained — in great detail, as Lady Meerka preferred specifics — what was happening.

"Odd," she had said after Danthres had laid out the case to date, "that a member of the royal family would decide instead to become a pirate, but I suppose it's also odd that a son of mine would conspire to take over the human lands. Regardless, this cook's accusation must be investigated, and the only manner in which that may be accomplished is to travel to Velessa and discuss it with Queen Marta and King Marcus."

"Well," the functionary was saying, "this is definitely Lady Meerka's seal, and I suppose that ridiculous armor you're wearing *might* be—"

"Lieutenants!"

Turning, Danthres saw a red-haired woman in gray leather armor, with a tree leaf emblazoned on the chest over his heart, and a bright green cape. She had a small scar over her left eye, and both eyes were the same green as the cape. They'd first met her at Lord Albin's funeral, where she had been part of the delegation of the Royal Guard sent to accompany the king and queen.

"Captain Andreja," Torin said. "It's good to see you again."

"I wish I could say the same, ban Wyvald — what happened to your beard?"

The functionary said, "Do you know these people, Captain?"

Andreja gave the functionary a look of disdain that Danthres admired tremendously. "Obviously, I do, Sir Stoora — and you should, too, at least by reputation. This is Lieutenant Torin ban Wyvald and Lieutenant Danthres Tresyllione of the Cliff's End Castle Guard."

Stoora shrunk a bit at Andreja's stare, but remained defiant. "The names mean nothing to me."

"I'll be sure to mention to the king and queen the next time I speak with them that their chamberlain has no knowledge of the two officers who broke the conspiracy against them a year ago."

Swallowing hard, Stoora said, "Oh, *them*! I had no idea!" He turned to face Torin and Danthres. "Forgive me, Lieutenants. I was away in Treemark on a family matter when the trial was going on, so I'm afraid I never had the privilege of meeting you in person."

Glancing at the letter from Lady Meerka, Andreja said, "I take it you're here on official business?"

Danthres nodded. "We need to have a *private* conversation with the king and queen at their earliest convenience."

"That will not be possible for several hours," Stoora said. Danthres noted that he'd shifted his tone to that of an efficient chamberlain attempting to do his job, rather than that of a pissed-off nobleman bitching about a stranger throwing up on his floor. "The king is currently in conference with Velessa's guild leaders, while the queen is attending the opening of a new bridge over the Gazrik River. Both of them have other commitments this afternoon as well that cannot be postponed. However, they were planning on having dinner alone together this evening. I will need to verify with them, of course, upon their return, but let us assume that they would not be averse to the pair of you joining them—if not for the meal itself, then for a drink afterward."

Danthres had gone into this expecting to have to fight to squeeze into the royal schedule, and had also expected to have to wait days. Knowing that they were likely to have their audience in a matter of hours was something of a surprise—and a relief.

"In the meantime," Andreja said, "this is an excellent opportunity for us to catch up. There's a dining hall for the Royal Guard here in the castle. Let us share a drink, and you can tell me the story of the evil demon who forced you to shave your magnificent beard."

Danthres laughed heartily.

"It was *not* a demon," was all Torin would say, though he didn't elaborate.

Belatedly, Danthres realized that in all the chaos of setting up this trip to Velessa yesterday and today, she never had a chance to speak with Torin about what happened between him and Jak at the Dog and Duck two nights ago.

Not wanting to leave Andreja hanging, but not wanting to air Torin's dirty laundry in public, Danthres said, "Torin is currently involved with someone who prefers him with less hair on his face."

"How absurd," Andreja said.

Stoora gave a half bow. "If you will excuse me, Captain, Lieutenants, I will speak with the chef and the steward about adding two to the royal meal this evening."

Danthres frowned. "What if they don't wish to dine with us, but see us afterward?"

"It is far simpler to subtract food and place settings from a meal than it is to add them. Should the king and queen choose to dine in private, you will simply eat the same food you would have eaten with them, albeit in the very dining hall to which Captain Andreja is taking you now."

"Thank you, Sir Stoora," Torin said. "We appreciate your efforts."

"Not at all." Stoora gave another bow. "It is the least I may do for the brave souls who saved the lives of our royal majesties."

With that, he departed.

Danthres watched him go, and said, "Dammit. He's taken all the fun out of taking an instant dislike to him."

Andreja chuckled. "Stoora's not that bad. He tends to overreact and put his foot in it, but he makes up for it later—he's a damn fine chamberlain, at the very least. Has this place running smoothly. C'mon, let's get a drink or four and you can tell me about this person who has the good taste to be romantically interested in you yet the bad taste to make you want to look like an imbecile."

Again Danthres laughed. Torin did so as well, though Danthres noted that it was subdued.

As Danthres had expected, the king and queen did not wish to give up their private dinner. She supposed that royalty had very few opportunities to be alone, and she wasn't about to deny them that, especially since they readily agreed to an after-dinner drink with the detectives.

They spent the rest of the afternoon with Andreja, getting a tour of the castle—their previous visits were limited to the areas where the trial was taking place—and being reunited with various members of the Royal Guard they'd met the previous year. Stoora also made arrangements for them to stay the night in guest quarters in the castle, allowing them a good night's sleep before being teleported home to Cliff's End in the morning, which pleased Danthres. Puking twice in one day was a bit much.

In the evening, they were treated to a superb meal of venison and rice, which they had to eat in the dining hall, to the envy of the Royal Guard, who never ate that well.

Once they'd finished eating, Danthres regarded her partner with concern. He'd been talking jovially with the Royal Guard during the day, but he'd been sullen whenever nobody was looking.

Nobody but Danthres, anyhow. Since they were no longer stuffing their faces and had to wait for Stoora or someone else to summon them into the royal presence, and since no one else was in the dining hall at present, she decided to finally have the talk that he'd promised a day and a half earlier.

"So—what happened at the Dog and Duck with Jak?"

Torin looked up suddenly, apparently surprised by the question. "I really don't think—"

"It could be hours before we're finally summoned. And if we're interrupted, then we'll pick it up later, but it's obviously troubling you."

Torin hesitated, then gulped some of the water that had come with the meal. After he swallowed, he again looked at Danthres. "I saw something in Jak I didn't like very much."

Then he told her of the events at the Dog and Duck, in particular Jak's use of the *bahrlan* slur.

"At first, he tried to pass it off as simply stress over losing the theatrical job, but then he used it again later in the evening when that poor bard got booed off the stage. Not," he added with a rueful smile, "that the bard didn't deserve it. He was well and truly horrible, but..." He sighed. "I've been seeing more and more ugliness directed at the refugees from Barlin, especially now that the initial sympathy for their plight has worn off. I fear that the city-state is turning into a powderkeg, and when it explodes, I don't know what side Jak will be on."

Danthres chose her words carefully, out of respect for Torin's feelings—Torin being pretty much the only person in all of Flingaria whose feelings she actually cared about enough to respect in the first place. "You should talk to him directly about this. Tell him of your discomfort, tell him of your concern."

Torin smirked. "And then throw the bigot out on his ass, which is what you wanted to say in the first place?"

Sighing, Danthres said, "Could you at least let me pretend to be considerate?"

"At the moment, I prefer the more typical Danthres who is blunt. But I do appreciate your consideration."

"Well, you *did* shave your beard for the man." Danthres grinned.

"I did. And I love the way he makes me feel, but—" He sipped more water. "It isn't just that, though. This job is the latest one that he's lost. He claims it's because they changed shows, but he's been let go from four consecutive jobs now. Once, twice even, I'm willing to accept poor circumstances, but four is a bit much."

Danthres considered Torin's words for a moment. "Tell you what— when we get back home, give me the information about those jobs. I'll investigate on my own, talk to the employers, see if there's a pattern to his being let go that he's not telling you."

"Or that he may not be aware of. He might be causing issues he doesn't realize are occurring—we've certainly seen that enough times." He put a hand on hers and clutched it with affection. "Thank you, Danthres. For the favor and for listening."

"Always, Torin, you know that."

A pageboy came into the dining hall. "'Scuse, but is you two the lieutenants from Cliff's End?"

"We are, yes," Torin said, getting to his feet.

Indicating the door with his hand, the pageboy said, "The king an' queen'll see you two now. Follow me."

Danthres let Torin go first, and then followed him and the pageboy out into the receiving room, up the winding staircase, and down the hall to a smaller dining room.

At the back of the room, facing the door, there was a huge table up on a raised platform, currently empty. There was space in the room for many smaller tables—Danthres could see scuff marks on the floor where the table legs normally were—but only one such table was in the very center of the room, at which the king and queen were seated. Two servants were bringing additional chairs to that table. The royal couple were facing each other, and the new seats were placed perpendicular to them.

The queen looked much the same as she had a year ago: ethereal, elegant, blonde. The king, however, had completely shaved both the small goatee he'd worn as well as the top of his head. Danthres recalled there were bits of gray last year, and she suspected he shaved rather than have the obvious signs of age on his person. Why he didn't use a glamour to cover it up, she had no idea.

Upon their entrance to the small dining room, the king looked over and smiled broadly. "Ah, Lieutenants, welcome! Please, join us." To the pageboy, he added, "Thank you, Lukass."

The pageboy nodded and beat a hasty retreat.

Danthres took her seat to the queen's left, while Torin sat to the king's left. "Thank you, Your Highness, for agreeing to see us," Torin said.

"No need to thank me," King Marcus said. "Even were it not on official business, the pair of you will always be welcome in this castle. I'm sorry we couldn't see you sooner, but affairs of state are never-ending."

Queen Marta asked, "But Sir Stoori has taken good care of you, yes?"

"He has, yes. As have your Royal Guard."

"Excellent," the king said.

A porter approached the table. "Would Your Majesties wish me to open a bottle of the new mead?"

"I believe so, yes, Harbart."

"Very good, sir."

Danthres generally hated mead, but wasn't about to refuse a drink with the king and queen.

"I see you shaved most of your beard, Lieutenant," the king said with a grin after Harbart went off to fetch the drink.

"And I see you shaved all of yours, Your Majesty."

The grin becoming a rueful smile, King Marcus said, "An experiment. The beard and hair softened my features as I age. I wish to look a bit more harsh."

"And less of a target," Queen Marta said.

"A forlorn hope, I admit," the king said. "The Silver Thrones will always be targets."

"As indeed they are right now," Danthres said.

Nodding approvingly, King Marcus said, "Down to business, then. Right. What is it you wish to discuss with us?"

Turning to face the queen, Danthres said, "First I must ask you a personal question, Your Majesty."

Queen Marta blinked in surprise. "Very well, Lieutenant. Given that it is personal, I cannot promise an answer."

Danthres did not reply to that caveat directly, but simply asked, "Did you have an older sister named Lillyana?"

The queen's lengthy hesitation and look of abject fear answered Danthres's question without her having to say a word.

Finally, though, the queen did speak. "I had a sister by that name once, but no longer."

"And you're aware that after she left Velessa she became a pirate, eventually becoming the legendary Pirate Queen?"

Slowly, Queen Marta nodded.

"Rumors have been circulating," the king said slowly, "that the Pirate Queen was murdered in Cliff's End. Is this true?"

Torin said, "She was actually murdered on the Garamin Sea, but her crew put in to Cliff's End and specifically requested that Lieutenant Tresyllione and I investigate her murder."

Danthres added, "I grew up in Sorlin, and the Pirate Queen often brought refugees to us from elf country. Her sailing master is an old friend, and—"

Suddenly the queen got to her feet and walked away from the table.

"Excuse me," the king said, and he also rose. Danthres and Torin, out of respect, also got up.

Danthres watched as King Marcus walked over to his queen and put a hand on her shoulder. She turned around and fell into an embrace.

After a few seconds, she palmed a tear from one eye, and said, "My apologies, Lieutenant. I had allowed myself to believe that the stories we'd been hearing of the Pirate Queen's death were just that—stories. I—I didn't wish to believe that my sweet Lillyana was dead."

"If you need some time—" Torin started.

"No," the queen said quickly. "You are investigating my sister's death, and I wish to do everything I can to aid you in that." She walked back to the table and sat down. The king did likewise, a look of grave concern on his face. Danthres saw that he really didn't want to continue this line of questioning until his queen had a chance to compose herself, but he wasn't about to gainsay her, either.

A knock on the dining room door signaled Harbart's return with the bottle of mead and four mugs, and the conversation ceased. Danthres assumed that this very private subject was not one the monarchs wished to have in front of anyone besides the two lieutenants.

Harbart poured each of them a drink—first the queen, then the king, then Danthres, then Torin—and took his leave.

After he was gone, the queen finally asked, "How did Lillyana die?"

"She was poisoned," Danthres said. "Since it did happen on open water, and since everyone on the *Rising Jewel* is accounted for, it has to be one of her crew."

The king sipped his mead and then asked, "Did her crew know she was Marta's sister?"

Danthres shook her head. "No, we learned of that from her cook—who is far more than a cook." She then outlined what Voran had told them about their Cabal.

Dryly, King Marcus said, "The pair of you have a knack for ferreting out conspiracies against our throne."

"I'm not entirely convinced the plural should be used, Your Majesty," Torin said. "Voran is from Iaron, and remember that Blayk spent his last few years living in Iaron. He said he was acting alone in his desire to rule the human lands, but that was never a particularly convincing claim. A plan as far-reaching as his requires an infrastructure."

"So you believe that Blayk was part of this Cabal?"

"Possibly. Or the Cabal is simply the latest iteration of the plot."

"Interesting."

"And," the queen added, "irrelevant. We're here to discuss my sister's death."

"They are related, Your Majesty," Danthres said. "Voran says he convinced Lillyana to return to Velessa and claim the throne, backed by the Cabal, and the following morning, she was found poisoned. I've no idea how much truth Voran is telling—my instinct says, not much, truth be told—but we needed first to verify that the Pirate Queen was indeed your sister."

"If Voran's story is true," Torin said, "then we have a job ahead of us, as all forty-five remaining crew on the *Rising Jewel* is suspect. As the Pirate Queen, your sister has committed quite the litany of illegal acts, and it is quite likely that a frightened outlaw pirate might view her becoming queen of the human lands to be akin to a death sentence—or, at the very least, a prison sentence."

Queen Marta took a long gulp of her mead, used a napkin to dab at the corners of her mouth, and then set her hands palms-down on the table. "I find it very difficult to credit this Voran person's story. Not the Cabal—that is depressingly likely—but rather that he convinced Lillyana to replace me on my throne."

Torin cocked his head quizzically. "May we ask why?"

"Because she did everything she could to avoid that particular responsibility." She took a deep breath. "Lillyana was two years older than I. From infancy, we were both trained in being members of the royal family, but where I was simply being shown how to be a noble, Lillyana was the one in line for the throne as the eldest. Everything there was to know about statecraft, about diplomacy, about decorum, about deportment, and about the responsibilities of being a monarch, she was shown.

"And she hated every moment of it." The queen chuckled. "She was genuinely interested in *some* of it, truly — the history, certainly, and diplomacy — but the rest bored her. She refused to take to her lessons, and deliberately sabotaged herself in them. When she reached her teen years, she came out and stated that she did not wish to be queen. By that time, my father realized that he needed a backup plan, as it were, so I was belatedly brought in to the royal training as well. I did decently at it, at least."

Placing his mead mug back on the table after gulping some, the king said, "My queen is far too modest. She was brilliant."

"I let others make such judgments," Queen Marta said with a shy smile at her king. Then her face grew serious again. "I was fifteen years of age, and Lillyana was seventeen, when my father took ill. While he lay sick, he pleaded with my sister, but her pleadings were even greater." Again she used her napkin, this time to dab her eyes. "I remember the conversation vividly. 'Please, Lillyana, think of the people,' Father said. And she replied, 'I am thinking of them, Father. I would make a terrible queen. Please, don't make me do what I am not fit to do. Marta is a beautiful soul and as noble a person as you will find in Velessa. She will rule our people with compassion and dignity — I fear all I shall do is annoy our allies and provoke our enemies.'"

"That sounds like the Captain," Danthres muttered.

"I beg your pardon, Lieutenant?" the queen asked archly.

"My apologies, Your Majesty. I knew your sister later in her life, and — well, that sounds very much like her."

"Yes, Lillyana preferred to do as she pleased. In truth, she would have made a fine leader, but a terrible ruler, as she was incapable of doing what she was told. And — as my husband can attest — there is no one in Flingaria who must do what they are told, rather than what they wish to, than a monarch."

"She was, in fact, a very fine leader," Danthres said. "Her crew is devoted to her—which is why it's so difficult to figure out which one of them killed her."

The queen nodded an acknowledgment to Danthres. "That does not surprise me. Lillyana was very charismatic. Everyone loved her. I think that's why Father was so disappointed that she rejected her birthright. In any event, Father was *very* insistent that, if she not take the throne after he died, that it be abundantly clear that she was abdicating her position as heir."

"I assume there's paperwork," Danthres said. There was *always* paperwork.

"Of the most binding kind, Lieutenant," the queen said gravely. "Before she left Velessa never to return, she signed a Fealty Contract to the Silver Thrones, with the Brotherhood of Wizards."

Danthres frowned. "I don't know what that is."

"I do," Torin said, "but only as a concept. I wasn't aware that such things actually were made."

"Oh, it's *very* real," King Marcus said, "and *very* rare. Primarily because it's also *very* expensive. Typical of magick."

Queen Marta nodded. "My father thought it worth the expense."

The look on the king's face indicated that he did not agree. The look of distaste on his face indicated a revulsion for magick that rivaled Danthres's—and hers was considerable. That may have been why he had avoided glamours to improve his appearance.

"What," Torin asked, "are the terms of the contract that Lillyana signed?"

"That she would make no claim to the Silver Thrones, that she rejected her birthright as the heir to King Tomsim, and that she would never set foot in Velessa again for all her days."

"And if she violates any terms of the contract?"

"A Misfortune Spell would be cast on her."

Torin's eyes widened. "I wasn't aware there was such a thing as a Misfortune Spell."

The king smirked. "Yes, well, it's not a spell they sell commercially, as the potential for chaos is tremendous. It's forbidden to be cast except on Fealty Contracts, and even then, it takes a wizard of tremendous power and with very expensive spell components to create it."

"Which," Danthres said, "would explain why it is such a pricey contract."

Nodding, the queen said, "However, what it does is give extremely bad luck to both the person the spell is directed at and anyone that person has affection for."

Danthres winced. "That would mean her entire crew would be affected—as well as, I assume, the pair of you," she added quickly.

"Not me," the king said. "We only met a few times. But my queen would definitely be adversely affected, at a time when she had already, in theory, lost her throne."

"Still, she would never risk that." Danthres finally gave in and took a sip of the mead. It coated her throat with honey and was far too sweet, but as mead went, it wasn't that bad.

There was a long, awkward pause after that. Danthres found she had no idea what to ask the monarchs next.

Luckily, the queen herself came to her rescue. "What is to become of her body?"

"We haven't addressed that, yet," Torin said. "At the moment, we've kept her crew confined to the *Rising Jewel*, along with the body."

"With respect," said Danthres, "I believe that her crew should have first say in the disposition of her remains."

"Of course." Queen Marta nodded. "However, there is a burial plot for the royal family here. If her crew would allow it, I wish her to be buried here. The Fealty Contract only affects her during life, and is now void."

Danthres blinked. "Wait, so it wouldn't affect any of her relations?"

"No. She was very specific that it only be directed at her, as she did not want any potential heirs to be denied a chance to be part of the royal family if they so wished. Why, does she have children?"

"She has a son, Rodolfo."

The queen looked at the king, who nodded. "If this Rodolfo wishes to come to Velessa and claim his place as a prince of the realm, he is welcome to do so. We will not challenge that."

Danthres suspected that Rodolfo would decline the honor, but it was his choice, at least.

She then looked at Torin, who nodded, and Danthres was amused that she and Torin had a silent communication similar to that of the two married monarchs.

"I believe that is all we need, Your Majesties," Torin said, getting to his feet. "We will not take up any more of your time."

However, the king waved his hand up and down. "Don't be absurd. Please, sit. Our business is concluded, but that doesn't mean we wish to be removed from your fine company. It is rare that we are able to get immediate impressions of the other city-states—it's generally rumors that are difficult to substantiate and reports we don't receive until months after the fact."

"Besides," Queen Marta added, "you have done us another great service today. Rarely does a day go by when I do not think of my wonderful sister. I have followed the Pirate Queen's exploits secretly—publicly, of course, we have always condemned her—but in private, I have enjoyed the tales of her adventures. In truth, I've always been envious. But I'm glad that you were able to confirm the truth of her demise to me. It would have been devastating to continue to hear those rumors for weeks until the official report came here."

"Of course." Torin sat back down. "It was our pleasure."

They spent several hours conversing after that, answering various questions about day-to-day life in Cliff's End, including the difficulties with Barlin refugees.

"We've had some people from Barlin also, but it's true, Cliff's End has borne the brunt," the king said after finishing off his mead. "Lord Doval might be well to consider some new laws."

"With respect," Danthres said, "I disagree. You can't legislate behavior, you can only punish it. But most of the behaviors being brought about by this hatred are already illegal. Possibly we could make punishments harsher, but that would only increase the population in Manticore Precinct."

"Perhaps." The king sounded thoughtful, but not entirely convinced.

"People dislike change," Torin said. "When everything is the same as it's been for a long time, they get comfortable. But when there's a major change, many people react badly. Any disruption they view as a personal insult."

"Then what do you suggest be done about this ill will toward the refugees?" King Marcus asked.

"Wait it out. It's possible that time will ease the tensions, as people adjust to the new reality. But we also need to be more vigilant. Lord Doval just opened a new precinct in New Barlin, which will help matters considerably. The Castle Guard was stretched far too thin to deal with the influx until a week ago. If matters grow worse even with the new precinct, then we should consider more drastic action."

Queen Marta nodded approvingly. "That is a very philosophical attitude, Lieutenant. Obviously, your training in Myverin has served you well."

Danthres assumed that the queen knew of Torin's home from his name.

Holding up his mug of mead in a toast, Torin said, "Thank you, Your Majesty."

The timechimes — which were higher pitched here than they were in Cliff's End — rang twenty-three, and before they were even finished, the king said, "I'm afraid that our lovely evening must cease now, as we must prepare for bed. Tomorrow, we see petitioners first thing in the morning, and that always requires a good night's sleep in advance."

"Of course." Torin rose, as did Danthres. "Thank you ever so much for your hospitality."

The queen also got to her feet, and gave them each a short bow. "The gratitude is ours, Lieutenants. You have done a great service to our kingdom today. And I wish you luck in finding the perpetrator."

"I believe," Danthres said, "that we have a fairly good notion who it is at this point."

SEVENTEEN

ALETA REALLY HATED IT WHEN THEY RAN.

It had started out so simply. They went to the boarding house on the River Walk with the giant fish on the door — the Becpar Arms. It was a large house with three floors and a huge wraparound patio. Aleta walked up the three stairs to the patio and knocked on the fish, while Dannee waited on the staircase up to the patio.

A dwarf answered the door. "What can I do for you, Detective?"

"I need to speak with one of your tenants, name of Xeros."

"Xeros, you say?" The dwarf suddenly started speaking in a louder tone. "I'm not sure if he's home. Maybe come back later?"

Aleta sighed. "What room is he in?"

"Not sure. I think it's one of the ones on the top floor, but — *uurrrrrrrk!*"

That last was all the dwarf could say once Aleta wrapped her hand around his neck. "Once more, what room is he in?"

From behind her, Dannee said, "Aleta, I hear a window opening on the first floor, around back."

"Top floor, hm?" She unceremoniously dropped the dwarf to the floor and went back out onto the patio. "Go around that way," Aleta said to Dannee, pointing to the west side of the house. She herself starting running around the east side.

"Right," Dannee said, and started moving that way.

Aleta ran around to see a person who looked just like the image in the crystal falling out a first-floor window.

"Xeros!" she cried out.

Without even turning to look, Xeros clambered to his feet and ran.

Aleta gave chase. She used to regularly identify herself as Castle Guard when she chased down someone she wanted to talk to, but after a month, she gave that up. They knew from the armor who she worked for, and they ran anyhow. So why waste breath?

The River Walk was the border between Goblin and Mermaid Precincts. Xeros jumped over the back fence to a building on the thoroughfare parallel to the River Walk. Undaunted, Aleta undid her cloak and let it drop to the ground and then followed suit — the cloak would just get in her way, and she could just say that she lost it while pursuing a murder suspect.

She leapt to the top of the fence that Xeros had had to climb to get to, then jumped down to a small yard.

Xeros was running between two houses toward Ferd's Way, a thoroughfare filled with shops. Aleta followed as Xeros weaved his way between the throngs of people walking up and down Ferd's.

Aleta just pushed her way through. Lots of people got out of her way at the sight of her Guard armor, but those who didn't, she shoved gently aside. Luckily, she knew her own strength, and she was able to use just enough force to move them without hurting them.

"Hey, watch it!"

"Stupid guard..."

"Get out of her way, y'shitbrain!"

Aleta ignored the shouting, did not waste energy shouting back or trying to importune the citizens of Cliff's End to help her stop a murderer. That way lay frustration and a lack of assistance, especially here in Goblin, so she just kept running, never taking her eye off Xeros.

He turned onto Phar Way, and Aleta smiled. That was a dead end, and the only structures there were whorehouses — low-cost ones for folks who couldn't afford the brothels on Sandy Brook Way — which weren't open at this hour, and a cobbler who'd gone bankrupt and whose store was shuttered.

Running into Phar Way, she saw Xeros pull up in front of the closed cobbler's, and turn around frantically. "Shit!"

Aleta stood with her hands on her hips. "Are we done with this idiocy?"

"I didn't do nothin'!"

"Yes, you did. You killed Soza Lambit in the Dancing Seagull. I'm arresting you for homicide."

"You can't do that!"

"Can't I?" Aleta said those words very quietly.

Xeros swallowed hard. "I mean, it ain't homicide when you kill a *bahrlan*. Worst that is is animal mutilation, or somethin'!"

"So you admit to killing him?"

"I —" Xeros hadn't realized that he'd caught himself up in a confession. "No, I mean, *if* I'd killed —"

Holding up a hand, Aleta said, "Please stop. Our magickal examiner cast a peel-back on the Seagull. He clearly saw you strangle Soza Lambit while the bar fight was going on. I don't suppose you started that?"

"Nah, but I woulda. I mean, the stupid *bahrlans* are all over the place! Sick of 'em. An' sick'a that Soza shitbrain, too. He got me fired from m'last job, complainin' 'bout my work! Where does some filthy *bahrlan* get off tellin' *me*, a loyal, tax-payin' citizen'a Cliff's End, how t'do my job?"

Aleta walked up to him and yanked his arms behind his back. "C'mon."

Of Dannee, there was no sign. Aleta sighed and headed back to where she'd last seen her partner, which was the boarding house.

Sure enough, as she approached — which took much longer, as she followed existing foot paths rather than jumping a fence, plus she was walking while encumbered with a prisoner, not running — Dannee stuck her head out the same window Xeros had crawled out of.

"Oh, good, you're back — and you got him!"

"No thanks to you," Aleta said. "Where were you?"

"Um, here." Dannee looked confused. "By the time I got around to the other side of the house there was no sign of either one of you. I don't run very fast, and I had no idea where you got to. So rather than wander around the area trying to find you, I figured it might be useful to investigate Xeros's room." She smiled. "And I was right. You should come in here. Oh, and I sent one of the youth squad to find a guard, so they can take him away."

Aleta's angry retort died on her lips. Everything Dannee had said was completely sensible. Yes, it would be good to have backup when chasing a prisoner, but only if that backup could actually assist. While Dannee's legs were much longer than that of a dwarf, they were on the short side by human or elven standards.

"Be right there." She dragged Xeros around to the front of the house and walked in the front door, pausing en route to pick up her cloak off the ground. She'd half expected it to have been stolen. At least now she wouldn't have to fill out any paperwork about losing it...

The dwarf who'd answered the door was in the hallway. "Ah, I see you caught him! Well done! I had no idea that a murderer was staying here, of course."

"Oh, I'm sure you didn't. You just figured he was a run-of-the-mill criminal, so you gave him a chance to leave without being arrested, thus forcing me to chase him down on foot, which I very much did not enjoy doing. Rest assured, I will remember that you made me do that the next time I need anything that relates to this boarding house of yours."

At that, the dwarf swallowed audibly and tried to shrink into the wall.

Out of the corner of her eye, Aleta caught Xeros mouthing a thank-you to the dwarf, to which the dwarf's only response was a scowl.

She entered the room, which was a basic boarding-house room: bed, water basin, desk. Not much by way of decoration.

Dannee held up a small stone encased in glass. "I found this on the desk. It has his name on it, as well as a date that I can only assume is his birth date."

Aleta shrugged. "Okay."

Realizing that Aleta had no idea of the significance of this stone, Dannee asked, "Do you know the history of Barlin?"

"Just that it was built on the plateau of Tserin's Peak."

Dannee winced. "No, that's Iaron."

Aleta sighed. She could never keep the other human city-states apart. "Fine, then I don't know the history of Barlin."

"It was founded as a mining colony at first, as there was a rich deposit of gold there. It's all tapped out, now, but there was a vein of pyrite that fooled people into thinking it was gold. Still, it's pretty, and about fifty years ago, a law was passed that every new child born in Barlin was given one of these stones. It was a source of pride for the city-state that their natives could have a token that showed that they were born in Barlin."

"Do you have one?" Aleta asked.

Dannee shook her head. "No, I wasn't actually born there. But he was."

Looking at Xeros, Aleta saw that he looked more than a little abashed. "You're *from* Barlin? You just went on at great length about 'bahrlans' and how awful they are, and you're one of them?"

"I am not! I came here on my own *years* ago! I ain't no stinkin' refugee!"

Brenn from Goblin Precinct came through the door. "There you are—got a message that one of you guys wanted us?"

Aleta practically threw Xeros toward the guard. "We did. Take this shitbrain to the hole. He's the one that committed the murder in the Seagull."

"Shouldn't he go to Mermaid, then?" Brenn asked.

"Technically, this boarding house is in Goblin, since it's on the north side of the River Walk, and besides, all of Mermaid's too busy keeping the gawkers away from the Pirate Queen. Just take him, please?"

"Fine fine, don't go strangling me in my sleep or nothin'."

As he left with the prisoner, Aleta called after him. "Keep making comments like that, Brenn, and I *will* strangle you, and I won't *wait* until you're asleep!"

"Look at that," Dannee said with a big smile.

Aleta turned to face her partner. "Look at what?"

"We just put our first case down together!"

That improved Aleta's mood tremendously. "We have, haven't we? Let's finish searching this room—"

"Oh, I've already searched it. There wasn't anything else of use. I mean, it's not like I'd find the murder weapon, since he used his hands."

"True." Aleta took one quick glance around the room just to be sure. "Fine, let's get back to the castle, fill out the paperwork, and then go get a drink at the Old Ball and Chain."

"Ooh, that'd be great! I've never been there!"

Aleta blinked. "How have you never been to the Chain?"

"I usually like to just go home after a shift. You know, relax and *not* see the same people I just spent half a day with. But for this? I'll definitely come out. In fact, I'll even pay for the drinks."

"Excellent." Aleta was going to offer to pay for the drinks herself, but if her new partner wanted to have that honor, she was not going to gainsay her.

The pair headed back toward Meerka Way.

EIGHTEEN

VORAN HAD BEEN RELUCTANT TO BE IMPRISONED IN THE DUNGEONS IN THE lower reaches of the castle, but as the lieutenants explained it to him, the alternative was to go back to *Rising Jewel*.

At this point, Voran suspected that he would not be welcome on the vessel, particularly based on the look Boatswain Rodolfo had been giving him ever since he volunteered to speak to the Castle Guard. He had lied and said that it was about business unrelated to the ship, but he didn't think Rodolfo believed it. In fact, Voran was sure that Rodolfo knew he was providing information about Princess Lillyana's death, and Rodolfo didn't seem pleased that Voran was telling the Myverin and the half-elf and not the other members of the crew.

But then, they weren't "other" members of the crew, truly. For all that Voran prepared their meals all this time, for all that they made requests of him for particular meals, he wasn't part of the crew. He pretended to be, of course, because that was his task, but it was over now. With Princess Lillyana dead, he had no reason to ever set foot on *Rising Jewel* ever again.

"I'm afraid," the Myverin had said, "that the only alternative to escorting you back to the Rising Jewel is to put you in a cell as a protected witness. We will make the cell as comfortable as possible—a consideration that actual prisoners do not get. For one thing, we might actually be able to give you a mattress."

"It's fine, Lieutenant," Voran had said, and he wasn't lying. Once the Myverin lieutenant had brought him to the cell, he'd laughed.

"Something amuses you?" the lieutenant had asked.

"In comparison to my cabin on *Rising Jewel*—which I share with three other people, and on which I sleep on a hammock that gives me motion sickness—this is positively luxurious."

He'd slept like a rock that first night, and then had been told by the guard that the lieutenants were in the midst of other business and would be back later. However, the guard had been authorized to bring him food, reading material, or other things he might like, within reason.

All Voran wanted was food and for this all to be over with.

"Later" turned out to be the following morning, when the guard unlocked Voran's cell and escorted him back up to the detectives' squadroom, specifically the same interrogation room where he'd been questioned two days earlier.

He waited there for some time before the two lieutenants finally entered.

"Good morning, good sir," the Myverin said. "Our apologies for keeping you in that cell for so long, but we had to investigate your claims."

That took Voran aback. "Excuse me?"

"We had to be sure," the half-elf said, "that your claims were true. After all, if we simply believed everyone who spoke in this room, no one in Cliff's End would have ever committed a crime."

Voran shifted in the uncomfortable stool he'd been sitting on. He hadn't expected that. "How—how did you—"

The Myverin smiled. "We travelled to Velessa. The Castle Guard has a wizard in its employ, you see, and he's more than capable of casting a Teleport Spell."

"I see." Voran hadn't expected this, but as he thought it over quickly, he realized it didn't matter much. He had been told there were records in Velessa of the princess's existence, and the lieutenants seeing them would only add validity to the Cabal's mission.

Not that it had a mission anymore. The princess's death negated their ability to install her on the Silver Thrones.

The Myverin sat in the chair opposite Voran, while the half-elf kept wandering about the room. It was very disconcerting, truly—she'd lean against a wall, then push herself off and wander to the other side, then lean against the door, then sit on the edge of the table that lay between Voran and the Myverin.

Trying not to let the half-elf's perambulations distract him, Voran cleared his throat and spoke. "I had a good deal of time to think in the cell you put me in—not much else to do, really..."

"Again, apologies," the Myverin said.

Holding up both hands, Voran said, "No, no, it's fine. As I said the other day, it was something of a luxury after a year on *Rising Jewel*. It's been some time since I've had that much privacy and quiet."

The Myverin glanced at the half-elf, currently inspecting her left glove while leaning against the door. "I do believe that's the first time the cells in the hole have been complimented for either of those aspects."

Voran chuckled. "You must not have had many sailors in here, then."

"Oh, we've had plenty," the half-elf said. "But they're not usually as talkative as you."

"Fair enough. In any case, I was thinking about who might be responsible for poisoning Princess Lillyana, and I keep coming back to the people I signed on with—the four refugees from that commune to the south."

"Sorlin, you mean," the half-elf said. She was now sitting on the edge of the table again.

"Right." Belatedly, Voran realized that, as a halfbreed, the lieutenant was likely at least familiar with Sorlin, if not actually from there. "Of course, you know of it. The princess travelled there often, I'm told, before it disbanded, and she regularly spoke very highly of the place." He smiled. "I suspect she would have liked both of you, in fact. She had a soft spot for halfbreeds, and she spoke often of how she envied the people of Myverin their lifestyle."

The Myverin scowled. "Most of those who envy the lifestyle of my homeland have never lived it. In any event, you mentioned that the Sorlin refugees were possible suspects?"

"Yes. You see, she favored those four quite a bit, especially the boatswain."

"So what?" the half-elf asked.

"Well, obviously, my entire plan was to take her away from the ship. They'd only been on board a year, and I suspect they signed up with the notion that they'd be serving under the legendary Pirate Queen for a lot longer than that. Finding out that she was leaving may have led one of them to kill her rather than allow that to happen. Honestly, my silver pieces would go on Rodolfo."

"Why him in particular?" the Myverin asked.

"He was next in line. Well, not next in line, but after serving on that ship for a year, I can assure you that neither the quartermaster nor the sailing master were going to take over. That puts the boatswain in position to take over."

"What makes you say that with regard to Chamblin and Lisson?" The half-elf was now pacing behind the Myverin.

"Nothing specific, they just seemed — I suppose, tired of it all. It felt to me as if they were only continuing to serve out of loyalty to Princess Lillyana. Had she been able to go through with our plan, they likely would have retired to some island on the Garamin with their accumulated ill-gotten gains."

"You suppose?" The half-elf stopped her pacing. "Didn't the Captain discuss it with you?"

"The disposition of her crew? No. I didn't really care about them all that much — my job was to convince her to claim her birthright."

"So you didn't discuss the crew," the Myverin said. "What did you discuss?"

"Excuse me?"

"Following our journey to Velessa, we now know the circumstances under which the Pirate Queen — or, as you say, Princess Lillyana — departed Velessa and ceded her claim on the throne to her younger sister. What we do not know is how you convinced her to reverse that decision."

Voran smiled. "It was easier than I had imagined."

"Was it?" The half-elf's question was dripping with sarcasm and doubt.

"No one was more surprised than I, Lieutenant," Voran said. "I had expected resistance, of course, but she was surprisingly amenable to the notion. She told me that she wasn't getting any younger and that gadding about the Garamin was, as she said, 'a game for children.' The notion of life in a castle, sitting on one of the Silver Thrones, was one she found very appealing as she grew older."

"Interesting," the Myverin said.

The half-elf finally sat down next to her partner. "Not especially."

"You don't believe me?" Voran asked. It was obvious that the half-elf didn't trust him, but at least the Myverin seemed to at least be considering what Voran was saying.

"I don't believe that the Captain never discussed what would happen to her crew with you. She was devoted to her crew and they to her."

"Absolutely," Voran said quickly. "However, from the moment I revealed my true nature, she no longer considered me part of her crew."

The half-elf nodded. "As well she shouldn't have."

Voran ignored her tone. "I have no doubt that she intended to take care of them."

"Interesting," the Myverin said again, "especially given what you said before."

Opening his mouth and then closing it in confusion, Voran just stared at the lieutenant. "What—what did I say before?"

"Your assumption was that whoever poisoned the Pirate Queen did so out of fear that, should she sit upon one of the Silver Thrones, she would condemn her former associates as pirates."

Again, Voran shifted on the stool. "I was merely speculating. Truly, all I may do is speculate—as I said, she didn't discuss that with me. Our conversations were focused entirely upon the process by which we would place her on the throne."

"And how exactly would you do that?" the half-elf asked. "You're aware, yes, that the king and queen have an army at their disposal? How would you get past the Royal Guard?"

"We wouldn't have to!" Voran chuckled. "Come now, Lieutenants, you said you went to Velessa so you know that Princess Lillyana's claim was completely legitimate. Our plan was no more complicated than to bring her to the castle and have her take her rightful place. We none of us want bloodshed, just an orderly transfer of power. Besides, violence would end poorly—people who try to kill the king or queen are boiled in oil, everybody knows that."

The Myverin leaned forward. "And the Pirate Queen was going along with this plan?"

"Yes. Our last talk the night before her food was poisoned was enthusiasm about going back to Velessa."

The half-elf got up again and started pacing. "That's the second time you've said that her food was poisoned."

Voran shrugged. "So?"

She stopped and stared right at him with her pitiless eyes. "How do you know that?"

Suddenly, Voran was completely confused. This had been going so well, with the entire interrogation going exactly as he'd rehearsed it for the past day in that cell.

This, though, was unexpected. "Everybody knows she was poisoned."

"Yes, that she was poisoned, but not her food. I mean," the half-elf added, "it could have been her food, but it also could have been a drink or placed in her mouth while she slept. Thanks to the wards the Captain put all over the ship, it was impossible for our M.E. to do a peel-back, and there was no evidence in her cabin of what killed her, so we don't know the specifics."

The Myverin leaned forward. "But you do."

Voran just stared at the two lieutenants for several seconds.

He thought he had accounted for everything. It never occurred to him that they wouldn't even know as much as when she was poisoned, only that she was poisoned. "I simply assumed that it was her food. Look, what difference does it make?"

"Quite a bit when you know the specifics of a murder that nobody else knows."

The half-elf smiled unpleasantly. "Usually such a person is, in fact, the murderer."

Voran laughed, and he hoped it didn't sound as desperate as he feared it did. "Why would I kill her? My entire mission was to bring her back! Our entire plan relied on her being alive!"

"No," the half-elf said, "actually, your entire plan relied on her being willing. And she wasn't."

"Excuse me?" This time Voran's laughter was derisive, and he meant it. "How could you possibly know what was in the princess's heart? You never even met her!"

"I haven't, no," the Myverin said, "but Lieutenant Tresyllione knew her quite well."

That brought Voran up short even more than the slip about the poison had. "You did?"

The half-elf sat back down and faced Voran. "I grew up in Sorlin. In fact, I was there when she brought Rodolfo to us. Indeed, that is why I was specifically requested to solve her murder, because Lisson and several other members of the crew know me."

Another mystery solved—Voran hadn't been present for those discussions-cum-arguments between the quartermaster and sailing master. He'd heard muffled yelling, but he'd no idea what it had been about, nor had he known why they set sail for Cliff's End and talked to these two in the first place.

The half-elf went on: "And one thing I know about the Captain is that she would never, under any circumstances, endanger the lives of her crew if she could possibly avoid it."

Now Voran was completely confused. "Of course she wouldn't. I think we can all agree on that, can't we, Lieutenant?"

"Are you familiar," the Myverin said suddenly, "with a Fealty Contract?"

In complete honesty, Voran replied, "No."

"It's a contract that's administered by the Brotherhood of Wizards," the lieutenant continued.

"Ah, that explains it." Voran leaned back and folded his arms. "I try to avoid dealing with wizards in general. Magick gives me a headache."

"Understandable," the half-elf said. "In this case, magick is what binds the contract."

"How so?" Voran asked, curious despite not having the faintest clue what this had to do with Princess Lillyana.

"If the any of the parties to the contract breaks any of the terms, the consequences are magickal in nature."

"As an example," the Myverin said, "a Misfortune Spell would be cast, causing the party as well as any of the party's loved ones to suffer eternal bad luck."

"Well, that's certainly a good reason to keep to a contract, but—"

"Like," the half-elf said as if Voran hadn't spoken, "the one Princess Lillyana signed."

Voran's reply died on his lips. "The—the what?"

"You see," the Myverin said, "when Princess Lillyana decided to cede her throne to Queen Marta, King Tomsim was dying. If she wasn't going to take over the throne, it needed to be, not just in writing, but unchangeable writing."

"Hence," the half-elf said, "the Fealty Contract."

"The only way that the Pirate Queen could have gone along with your Cabal's plan would be to violate that contract—which would cast a Misfortune Spell on her and everyone she loved."

The half-elf leaned forward. "Which means she would never, under any circumstances, go along with your plan." She leaned back and smirked. "Well, unless she wanted to fail as the queen of the human lands, since the Misfortune Spell would be disastrous for everyone—but it would also affect everyone she loves, from her crew on down."

Voran said nothing. He dared not speak another word. They had known about this Fealty Contract since the questioning started. They'd let him weave out the entire tapestry of the lies he'd told to cover his own failure.

Though at least now the failure made sense. The stupid princess simply would not say why she wouldn't go along with it—he was even willing to accept her refusal if it came with a good reason, but she never provided one. If she'd just *said* she'd signed one of these be-damned Fealty Contracts, he would have been on his way. But no, she just refused, and Voran couldn't—*could not*—go back to the Cabal with an out-and-out rejection that was not backed up by a solid basis.

Had he known about that be-damned contract, he never would have poisoned her and set up one of the others to be framed for it. It had been such a good plan. The others should have devolved into chaos as they tried to figure out who did it, and Voran would have eventually snuck off and headed back to Iaron. If anyone had pressed him, he would have told as much of the truth as he'd told these lieutenants: he was the last person who would have wanted Princess Lillyana dead.

But he said none of this.

"Have you nothing to say all of a sudden, Cook?" the half-elf asked with a sneer.

"No."

"Very well." The half-elf got to her feet. "We'll take you back to the hole—without the mattress this time—and in the morning, the magistrate will condemn you to boil in oil."

Voran coughed. "What?"

The half-elf stared down at him. "People who kill members of the royal family are boiled in oil. Everybody knows that."

"But—"

The Myverin had also risen. "I'm surprised you didn't realize the consequences of your action. I suppose you might be able to argue that she wasn't a member of the royal family at the time you killed her— what with the Fealty Contract and all—but you didn't know about that, and you killed her knowing full well what her bloodline is, so I can't imagine the magistrate will accept that argument."

Putting his head in his hands, Voran felt his stomach churn and his forehead break out in a sweat. He hadn't expected to get caught, but even if he had, he figured he would be hanged like a civilized murderer. But boiled in oil? That sounded so very—painful.

"Of course," the half-elf said, putting her hand to her chin, "he could possibly plea for a lesser sentence."

"That would require him to give up his fellow members of the Cabal," the Myverin said. "I can't imagine he would do that."

"True."

Voran just sat there in the interrogation room long after the two lieutenants left, until some guard came to take him back down to the cell.

As promised, the mattress was gone. So was the food tray and the reading material. He had no idea when his next meal would be, and the guard who was so friendly earlier wouldn't speak to him now.

He was doomed. He'd messed up so very badly, and the only way to avoid being boiled alive was to give up his friends and associates.

Was it worth it? He'd probably be hanged either way, so he'd be just as dead.

Unwilling to make that decision without serious consideration, he lay down on the now-much-more-uncomfortable bunk to consider his options.

Voran believed in the Cabal's cause. He did. Truly.

But was there even a cause left? Elevating Lillyana to the throne was the only way to accomplish their goals quickly and bloodlessly. The backup plans were either long-term or violent—or both. Voran had volunteered for this mission precisely because it was neither of those things.

Was it worth avoiding the bloodshed that would surely follow now that Princess Lillyana was dead to betray his friends—and give himself a less painful death?

As he set his head down on the cot, he found himself with no clear answers.

NINETEEN

"It amazes me that all this time she was the queen's *sister*."

Chamblin said those words while sitting in the mess hall on the *Rising Jewel*. With the Pirate Queen's killer now incarcerated and awaiting the magistrate's judgment, Danthres had asked Boneen to remove the wards, which made the quartermaster happy, as it allowed the boat to sail out into the open sea and away from the gawkers on the docks, which made Sergeant Mannit happy.

Danthres and Torin had joined Chamblin here in the mess hall, along with Lisson and Rodolfo. The two lieutenants had boarded the pirate vessel after Boneen removed the wards, and sailed with them out into the Garamin Sea. Once they'd dropped anchor far enough away that they couldn't be seen from the docks, the five of them had gathered to discuss what would happen next.

Lisson asked, "What will happen to Cook?"

"Never liked him much," Chamblin said. "Never liked his food or him."

"Just last week you were calling him the best cook we'd ever had!"

"I never said that!" Chamblin folded his small arms over his tiny chest.

Rodolfo smiled. "You did, actually."

"Regardless," Danthres said before Chamblin and Lisson devolved into *another* argument, "to answer Lisson's question, Voran will go before the magistrate. If he gives up the rest of his little Cabal, he might get an easier sentence. If he doesn't, he'll likely be boiled in oil."

Rodolfo's face scrunched into an unpleasant frown. "Do the king and queen really *do* that? I though that was just to scare people."

"They did it to Lord Blayk last year," Torin said.

Lisson nodded. "Two conspiracies in one year, I can see why they'd want the nastiest penalty."

"Actually, this is likely the same conspiracy," Torin said. "But that's an issue for the authorities in Velessa and Iaron. If we're fortunate, Voran will forego an agonizing death in exchange for his fellows."

"If we're not fortunate," Danthres said with a sigh, "he'll be boiled and then we'll have to wait and see what their *next* scheme is."

Torin said, "Meantime, you'll need to find another cook."

"Possibly." Chamblin glanced at Lisson, who glanced back.

Danthres recognized the exchange of looks between two people who knew each other very well. She and Torin had spent the last eleven years perfecting similar looks, not to mention watching the king and queen do the same thing at Castle Tomsim. "What is it?"

"The fact is, I'm not sure there is even to be a ship after this."

Rodolfo's eyes went wide. "What?"

Chamblin sighed. "I'm tired, Rodolfo. Tired of sailing up and down the Garamin, tired of everyone either being in such awe of us that they do nothing but gawk — like those shitbrains in Cliff's End — or so frightened of us that they try to kill us as soon as look at us. I'm tired of charting courses, I'm tired of scheming, I'm tired of all of it."

"And I'm also tired'a *him*," Lisson added with a good-natured smirk. "Only reason the two of us haven't killed each other is thanks t'the Cap'n. Without her, s'only a matter of time 'fore we strangle each other."

Chamblin laughed. "Days, I'd say."

"But yeah," Lisson said, "I'm tired, too. I've only stayed this long outta loyalty to the Cap'n. Now? I just wanna retire to a life'a leisure. That's what we're all aiming toward in any case — no point in acquiring ill-gotten gains if you can't spend 'em."

"I'd say the same is true for well-gotten ones," Torin said. "And based on what I understand of your hierarchy, Rodolfo, that would make you next in line to captain the *Rising Jewel*."

Silently, Danthres marveled at the irony that the very motive Voran had falsely ascribed to Rodolfo for poisoning the Captain might wind up being the result of Voran's own poisoning of her. She also noted that Voran's observation about Chamblin and Lisson's desire to remain as pirates without the Captain was completely accurate. Aloud, she said, "Before you comment on that, Rodolfo, there's something you should know."

Rodolfo grinned. "In the last several days, the Captain was killed, I found out she was my mother, and then found out that she was also the older sister of Queen Marta. I'm not sure I can handle too many more revelations, Thressa."

"And by the way," Chamblin grumbled, "I still can't believe the Captain kept that from us."

"She wanted it that way," Lisson said.

Chamblin pointed a tiny finger at Lisson. "I especially can't believe that *you* knew and *I* didn't! I'm her damned second-in-command, I should've—"

"It had nothin' t'do with that, Chamblin, an' you know it! You weren't signed on yet when Rodolfo was born!"

"You were just a deckhand, and *you* knew of it!"

"Kinda hard t'miss the Cap'n bein' pregnant! Not to mention hidin' out for most'f a year. But she didn't want no one else knowin', so she swore us all t'secrecy. Gotta admit, I thought it was strange when he signed on last year, but I talked to the Cap'n about it, an' she said he was a good sailor with good references—and no one else'd take 'im after *Letashia* anyhow." He shook his head. "Stupid sailors."

"There, I'll agree," Chamblin said. "We got more good sailors that way, though. When no legit boat'll hire you 'cause you survived a wreck, we're a place to go."

Grateful that the pair of them had worked their way out of the argument without her having to break it up, Danthres said, "In any event, we told King Marcus and Queen Marta about you."

"Really?"

"You sound surprised," Danthres said.

Rodolfo looked away. "I am. I'm not sure they'd appreciate such a reminder."

"Despite her chosen way of life," Torin said, "I inferred no embarrassment or anger regarding your mother from Queen Marta. She spoke of her sister only with love, affection, and regret."

Danthres added, "And King Marcus specifically said that, if you wish, you are welcome to travel to Velessa and claim your place in the royal family."

"Ha!" Lisson grinned. "From boatswain to pirate prince to prince of the realm in less than a week!"

Chamblin just grumbled something incoherent, and Danthres feared another argument between the Captain's lieutenants.

"What about the Fealty Contract?" Rodolfo asked.

"It only applies to her," Torin said. "Your mother didn't wish any potential offspring to be beholden to a choice she made."

"That certainly sounds like her," Chamblin said. "She may've been a secretive little schemer, but she was always a fair one."

"She was less secretive than most," Rodolfo said. "In fact, she was far more open and generous than most so-called 'legitimate' ship captains. I also think that she had a plan for me, and only didn't tell me because of that fairness. She wished me to choose my own path, but she also did what she could to clear that path." He blew out a breath. "To that end, as much as I am honored by King Marcus's offer to actually be his nephew, I think my place is on *Rising Jewel*, continuing my mother's work."

"Better a pirate prince than a prince of the realm, then?" Torin asked with a smile.

"I believe so, yes." He turned to the other two. "The question is, if the pair of you are truly retiring?"

"Absolutely," Chamblin said.

"As soon as possible," Lisson added.

Rodolfo smiled. "Just so. Therefore, do you think the crew would accept me as the new captain?"

The pair exchanged knowing glances again.

Lisson finally said, "I think we should tell the crew that you're the Cap'n's son, first. It'll be a relief t'those of us who've been keepin' it quiet all these years, for one thing."

Chamblin nodded in agreement. "We'll speak for your worthiness to take over. Between that and your being the Captain's actual heir, I suspect that most follow your leadership."

"Assuming, of course, that the rest of the crew don't follow the pair of us into retirement."

Danthres got to her feet. "We will leave you to that, then."

Lisson also rose. "Thank you, Danthres. And you as well, Lieutenant," he added with a glance at Torin, who had also gotten up. "I know that the Cap'n woulda wanted it this way—I mean, not t'have been killed. But if she *was* killed, I think she woulda wanted you t'be the one to solve it."

Chamblin did not get up, but he sounded sincere when he said, "And you did solve it, for which you have my gratitude."

"And mine, as well," Rodolfo said. "Assuming the crew accepts me and I do take command, you can rest assured that, should you ever need a favor, *Rising Jewel* will be at your disposal."

"Thank you for that," Torin said. "And also thank you for what you have shown me these past few days."

"What is that?" Rodolfo asked.

Danthres had been about to ask the question herself, as this was not something she had expected her partner to say.

"I came to this case with a certain prejudice toward those of your vocation. I had many encounters with pirates during the elven wars — not your Captain, mind you, but others. As Danthres can attest, I was disdainful of you all. I will confess that I still do not think well of your choice to exist outside the law. As a former philosopher of Myverin, as a former soldier in the human army, and as a current detective in the Cliff's End Castle Guard, I fight for order, where your very existence foments chaos. But one of the things that all three of those occupations have also taught me is not to assume and not to prejudge. Particularly as a detective, I should have put my own issues to one side and focused instead of closing the case. What you have all shown me, in our interviews about the Pirate Queen, and in the loyalty you have all shown for each other, is that, while I may not find nobility in your purpose, there is a great deal of nobility in your community. Your support of your fellows is impressive, and the life you have made for yourselves is to be admired."

"Thank you, Lieutenant," Lisson said. "I gotta admit, I felt that disdain you mentioned pretty damned hard when you first came to talk t'me. Gladja could see our side'a things."

Chamblin added, "And glad you could find the murderer. Still say Cook was always a piece of shit."

"Oh, cut that out, Chamblin," Lisson said.

Rodolfo guided Torin and Danthres toward the mess hall entrance. "Let us depart before the pair of them come to blows. I will return you to the docks on our dinghy personally. That will give the pair of them a chance to finish arguing and figure out how they'll tell the crew about me."

Torin chuckled. "I doubt those two will ever finish arguing. They're like to retire to the same place so that they may continue the fights until one of them dies."

Danthres waited until they were on the dinghy and bound for Cliff's End before asking the question she needed to ask the son of the Pirate Queen. "Are you sure this is what you want, Rodolfo?"

"I'm a sailor, Thressa. Even when I was a boy in Sorlin, I was always gazing out at the reefs. A life of sitting in a castle would, I suspect, bore me to tears. The sea is where I'm meant to be, and besides—what better way to carry on the Captain's legacy?"

"The bards are going to have a field day with this," Torin said with a grin.

"Definitely." Danthres chuckled.

"I STILL CAN'T BELIEVE SHE WAS THE QUEEN'S *SISTER*."

Aleta sighed. Captain Dru had been saying that about once an hour since Torin and her partner had returned from Velessa that morning with confirmation that the Pirate Queen's cook's allegations about her parentage was correct. He said it now in response to the two lieutenants returning from the pirate ship.

"She really was," Tresyllione said with a smile. "But there are no new claimants to the Silver Thrones. Rodolfo will be remaining aboard the *Rising Jewel*."

"Good," Dru said emphatically. "I don't think I could handle another attempt on the king and queen."

Dannee, who was standing behind Aleta observing her filling out the report on their case, said, "Wow, that's amazing."

"What's amazing?" Aleta asked.

"Well, Lieutenant Tresyllione and Lieutenant ban Wyvald have solved the murders of Gan Brightblade *and* the Pirate Queen! That's amazing!"

"First of all," Torin said, "it's Danthres and Torin, Dannee. You need no longer refer to us by rank."

"Oh! But you're senior detectives! So you outrank us!"

"No," Tresyllione said, "it just means we get paid more."

Dru chuckled. "Mostly 'cause they do stuff like solve the murders of Gan Brightblade an' the Pirate Queen. Not t'mention the first time anybody committed homicide on a wizard."

"Someone killed a *wizard*?" Dannee asked, shocked.

Aleta rolled her eyes. The last thing she wanted to hear was a litany of the halfbreed's accomplishments. But that was her lot in life, as Dru said, "No, someone killed *three* wizards. It was their first case together. I was still a guard back then, an' everyone all over town was talkin' about it. An' then they took down Quanto—"

"Please stop." Tresyllione looked pained. Aleta was pleased to see that she was just as uncomfortable with the approbation.

"Hey, I'm captain now, I can say what I want. For now, though, I'm just gonna say good job closin' it fast and gettin' that boat the hell out." He turned to Aleta. "You two done with your report yet?"

"Ah," Torin said, "in all the dashing back and forth, I never did find out—you tracked down the killer from the Seagull?"

"We did!" Dannee said enthusiastically. "It actually went very smoothly! After Boneen did the peel-back, we showed the image to the victim's brother, he recognized the face, and pointed us at someone who might know where to find him."

"Palnitt," Aleta added helpfully.

Tresyllione got a gleeful look on her face. "Oh, please tell me he resisted and you had to intimidate him?"

"Aleta did, yes," Dannee said.

"Of course. Excellent. Wish I'd been there to see it. Well done."

That got Aleta to squirm a bit in her seat. Praise from the halfbreed was—unusual to say the least.

"She was very good at it," Dannee said. "Anyhow, he claimed he killed the victim because he didn't like refugees from Barlin—except it turns out *he* was from Barlin originally, too! Not a refugee, though, he moved here a while ago."

"Lord and lady, this is getting ridiculous," Tresyllione muttered.

"Agreed," Torin said. "Let's hope opening the new precinct will make a difference."

Dru nodded. "Well, the first few days of Phoenix Precinct have been pretty quiet. Lot less stuff reported in New Barlin to Phoenix than Dragon and Goblin were gettin' before, but that's prob'ly just 'cause they're all scared'a the new set'a guards in town. We'll see if it sticks. Anyhow, four'a you're all back in rotation—'less the magistrate needs you two?"

Torin shrugged. "We'll find out in the morning, but I doubt it."

"Unless he makes a deal," Tresyllione added. "But I'm with Torin, I doubt it. Voran doesn't strike me as self-centered enough to make that deal. I mean, he's an Iaron noble, and he gave that up to be a cook on a pirate ship for a year—all for a cause. He won't give in now, even to keep from being boiled in oil."

"Perhaps." Aleta rubbed her chin. "It's my experience that people will do anything to avoid great pain."

"People, yes. Fanatics, no. Voran's a fanatic."

Before Aleta could argue the point further—in her days with the Shranlaseth, fanatics were often the ones who broke first—Manfred and Kellan entered the squadroom looking incredibly dejected.

Dru stared at them. "I'd ask how it's goin', but the looks on your faces kinda tell me that already."

Manfred held up his hands. "We give up. We have talked to every single person who may or may not have had a grudge against every single person who was vandalized. If any of them did it, they're hiding it real good, and we can't find a damn piece of evidence to support it. Nobody's seen the graffiti being painted on, and nobody's done any since we started investigating."

"Personally," Kellan said, "I think that the artist gave up soon as he saw we were on the case."

"Or he couldn't afford any more Invisibility Spells," Manfred said.

"That's his theory." Kellan jerked a thumb at his partner.

Manfred put his hands on his hips. "Yeah, it's my theory, you got a problem with that?"

"All right, stop!" Dru held up a hand. "You two satisfied that you pursued all the leads?"

"We got nothin', Cap." Manfred hung his head.

"Okay, unless somethin' else comes up, you two're back in the rotation."

Tresyllione pumped a fist and looked at Torin. "Yes! You owe me a copper!"

Chuckling, Torin reached into the pouch on his belt and fished out a copper piece, flipping it to the halfbreed, who caught it unerringly.

Manfred looked annoyed. "You two were betting on our streak? That's rude."

"Nice try, partner," Kellan said. "That's two silvers."

"Get me at payday."

Aleta had never been able to understand the notion of wagering on police work—it was the one aspect of working for the Castle Guard she had never quite been able to wrap her mind around—but while she could at least understand Torin and his partner betting on Manfred and

Kellan's streak, the pair of them betting on it was a bit more confusing to her. "Wait, Kellan, you bet on your streak ending?"

Kellan grinned. "Not exactly. Manfred told me that he could feel it in his bones that the streak'd hit twenty, and he put two silvers on it. No way I *wasn't* gonna take that action."

"Smart man," Torin said.

The timechimes rang signaling the end of the shift.

Dru looked up and said, "Damn, where'd the time go? All'a you, go home. You all did good today."

"We did?" Dannee asked.

"Sure. You an' Aleta put down a murderer, Torin and Danthres put down another murderer, an' Manfred an' Kellan reminded us that we ain't perfect. Go home."

Dannee said, "I already offered to buy drinks for Aleta and myself in honor of closing our first case together, and I'm happy to extend that to any of the rest of you who are coming along."

"Actually," Tresyllione said, "it seems to me that the two detectives who've spent the last several weeks going on at nauseating length about their oh-so-amazing streak, and whose aforementioned streak was unceremoniously broken today, should be the ones to pay for the drinks at the Chain."

Aleta surprised herself with the words, "I agree!"

"As do I," Torin said. "And if it's a notion that both Aleta and Danthres agree upon, then it is a worthy notion, I would say."

"Hell," Dru said, "I was gonna stay and do paperwork, but if Kellan an' Manfred are buyin', I'm in, too."

Aleta looked at the two detectives in question, who both looked completely stunned, mouths hanging open.

Kellan recovered first. "Whaddaya think, partner? Streak had to end eventually. And hey, at least we *had* the streak. That's worth a few drinks, right?"

Manfred shook his head and laughed. "Yeah, I guess. Fine, drinks're on us!"

"Excellent," Aleta said. "Dannee and I will catch up to you, we just have to finish the report on the Lambit case."

"Do it in the morning," Dru said. "Magistrate's gonna be dealin' with Voran first thing, so he ain't gonna get to Xeros for a while. 'Sides, you're off the clock now. Nobody should be doin' paperwork 'less they're gettin' paid for it."

It went against all of Aleta's training to leave a job half finished. But Dru was both her former partner and her boss, and she wasn't about to argue with him. "Very well."

"Wait," Manfred said to Dru, "you said you were gonna stay and do paperwork."

Dru scowled. "Yeah, that's the downside'a bein' a captain. I ain't never off the clock. I get paid the same no matter how many hours I work."

"That sucks."

His scowl turning into a grin, Dru said, "Yeah, but I get paid more'n you. C'mon, let's go drink."

"I'm all for that," Tresyllione said.

"I'm afraid I must pass," Torin said. "I'm going to be seeing Jak."

"Bring him along," Dru said. "Let Manfred and Kellan buy his drinks, too."

"Hey!" Kellan said.

Torin chuckled. "No, it's fine. We need some time alone. I'll see you all tomorrow."

As Torin left, Aleta watched as Tresyllione looked upon her partner's departure with obvious concern.

She decided to actually talk to her. After she got up from her desk, leaving the paperwork half-finished, and retrieved her cloak, she approached the halfbreed. "Is he okay?"

Tresyllione sighed. "I'm honestly not sure. Ask me again tomorrow morning."

"I suspect I won't have to." Aleta smiled. "Your partner wears his emotions on his sleeve."

"True." She indicated the door. "C'mon, Shranlaseth, let's go get extremely drunk."

Aleta's eyes widened. "Extremely drunk? Why so much?"

Smiling, the halfbreed said, "Because Manfred and Kellan are paying for it, obviously. One should always drink as much free booze as one can."

Dannee laughed. "That sounds like a fabulous philosophy, Lieutenant. Sorry! Danthres!"

Aleta walked out with Tresyllione on one side of her and her new partner on the other side, and she had to admit to kind of liking that.

"YOU MEAN TO TELL ME SHE WAS THE QUEEN'S *SISTER*?"

Torin nodded at Jak's question. They were seated on a bench in the dock extension, arms around each others' shoulders, looking out at the darkened sea, flickering torchlight providing illumination. During the day, the bench was used by construction workers when they took their meal breaks. At night, the area was closed—especially now that the *Rising Jewel* had left—but the guard, an old Castle Guard lifer named Byron Mazz, let Torin and Jak in. It was probably the only place in all of Cliff's End where one could truly be alone outdoors these days.

"Hope Medinn finds out about it when he finally shows up," Jak said with a chuckle.

"I'm sure he's already heard. Word of the Pirate Queen's death had already reached Velessa by the time we arrived, and we teleported."

"Well, this will certainly add to your legend, Lieutenant ban Wyvald." Jak smiled and rested his head on Torin's shoulder. "Obviously, you're the person to go to when a legend is killed."

"Personally, I'd rather close cases involving ordinary people—they're less work. And require less teleporting and watching Danthres throw up."

"I can't imagine that's very salubrious, no." Jak raised his head. "Are you all right, Torin? You seem—out of sorts. Usually after you close a case, you're relaxed."

"This case has brought out some ugly emotions in me," Torin said. "When we first boarded the *Rising Jewel*, I was harsh to the crew. I'd pre-judged them, assuming that their lifestyle meant they were reprobates. I was looking for excuses not to take the case."

"You didn't need to look for an excuse," Jak said. "The Pirate Queen wasn't murdered in Cliff's End."

"No, but they wanted Danthres to solve it as a favor. Because Danthres was her friend. And that should have been enough for me. I know how rare it is for Danthres to consider someone to be a friend."

Jak grinned. "You being among that miniscule number."

"Exactly." Torin sighed. "I should have been happy for her. You should've seen her, Jak—I haven't seen her so at ease with *anyone* besides myself in eleven years as she was with Lisson and Rodolfo. And the way she spoke of the Pirate Queen—she called her 'the Captain,' the same as the crew did—it was with a nostalgic reverence. More to the point, it was with love. Danthres has loved very little in her life, and taking on this case was obviously important to her."

Torin pulled himself out of their mutual embrace and got to his feet, suddenly feeling the need to pace.

"It should have been more important to me. But I couldn't get past my own disdain." Torin sighed. "I saw so many horrible things done by pirates during the war."

"Your reaction makes sense."

Torin turned to face Jak. "But it doesn't, don't you see? I never encountered the Pirate Queen before this week. I made a judgment based solely on people who happen to be in the same profession. I had thought myself above such things."

Jak scowled, looking up at Torin. "And you thought me above them, too?"

Torin sat back down and looked into Jak's beautiful dark eyes. "That's not what I'm talking about, Jak, I—"

Jak looked away. "Isn't it? You've been out of sorts ever since I used that damn word. I can't help it, I keep hearing it all over town. 'Lousy *bahrlans*,' 'filthy *bahrlans*,' 'everything was fine until the *bahrlans* showed up.' It starts to affect you."

"I know it does. And that's why I'm *not* talking about you here. I'm talking about my own instinctive reaction to treat the *Rising Jewel* crew with scorn, which is the same as your own instinctive reaction to using that term—and, more to the point, agreeing with the dismissive and reductive treatment of the refugees that that term implies."

Jak rolled his eyes. "Oh, Wiate's foot, there's that Myverin education again."

"I thought you liked it when I got all brilliant on you," Torin said bitterly. Then he softened his tone. "And why Wiate's foot?"

"Because I hadn't done his foot yet." Now Jak got to his feet and started pacing. "Look, Torin, I'm sorry I'm not the paragon of virtue that you are. In my defense, neither is anyone else. Maybe the reason why you've been unable to sustain a relationship is because nobody can live up to your lofty standards."

Torin stood up and put his hands on Jak's shoulders. "I'm not asking you to. I'm sharing a moment of self-examination with someone I love. That's all."

Jak just stared at Torin for a moment. The breeze picked up off the Garamin and blew his hair into his face.

"So this wasn't a veiled attempt to get me to apologize for what happened at the Dog and Duck?"

"I will never 'get' you to do anything, Jak. You're a person with free will, and I love you for who you are, prejudices and all."

"I guess I'm not used to falling for paragons of virtue." Jak chuckled. "But I'd like to try to get used to it, if you're willing."

"What makes you think I wouldn't be?"

"Well, honestly, I thought you took me out here to break up."

Now it was Torin's turn to stare at Jak uncomprehendingly. "Why would I do that?"

"In case I caused a scene, here it would be in private and not embarrass you."

"If I ever do decide to break up with you, Jak, there will be no subterfuge or manipulation. I detest such things."

"Like any good paragon of virtue." Jak finally put his own arms on Torin's shoulders. "Forgive me for thinking that you'd be just like everyone else I've been involved with? They all tried to manipulate my emotions, and it grew tiresome. I guess I've come to expect people to think badly of me once they get to know me."

"Well, I don't. I wish this relationship to continue. Besides, I'm invested—I shaved my beard for you!"

Jak made a face. "And a good thing, kissing you with it was *awful.*"

Torin threw his head back and laughed. "Indeed. However, there is one thing I wish to hear from you."

Cautiously Jak asked, "What's that?"

"Tell me the significance of Wiate's foot."

It was Jak's turn to laugh. He leaned forward and kissed Torin, and then guided him to the bench.

Torin listened with contentment as Jak spun a tale about the power of the god Wiate's foot. "Specifically the right one," Jak made sure to emphasize. "The left one was shit."

They continued to sit on the bench long into the night.

THE END

BONUS VIGNETTES

Since December 2017, Keith R.A. DeCandido's Patreon (which you can support at patreon.com/krad) has included monthly vignettes featuring his original characters. In the first year of the Patreon's existence, four of those vignettes have featured characters and situations from the "Precinct" series, and as an added bonus, we present those four mini-tales for you here in Mermaid Precinct.

"An Unexpected Trip to Sandy Brook Way" features Danthres (reluctantly) talking to Suzett, the owner of one of the prostitution houses on that thoroughfare, in a story that takes place prior to Dragon Precinct.

Both "Don't Ask the Question if You Don't Want the Answer" and "The Streak" take place in the year between Gryphon Precinct and Mermaid Precinct, the former involving the newest members of the detective squad, the other showing Manfred and Kellan in the early days of their record-breaking streak as seen in Mermaid Precinct.

And then we have "Gan Brightblade and the Swamp of Kormak," a tale of Brightblade and Bogg the Barbarian, two of the heroes who were victimized in Dragon Precinct, from their days as adventurers.

An Unexpected Trip to Sandy Brook Way

"What can I do for you, Detective?"

Lieutenant Danthres Tresyllione of the Cliff's End Castle Guard gritted her teeth at Suzett's words. The woman who ran the brothel in a cul-de-sac on Sandy Brook Way wore a scoop-necked dress that accentuated considerable cleavage. Wrinkles had started to become visible on her smooth face, which meant she didn't use a glamour, unlike her employees. She stood in front of the beads that hung from the entryway to a back room off the brothel's main foyer. Danthres assumed it to be her office.

Lieutenant Torin ban Wyvald, Danthres's partner, usually dealt with Suzett, as she'd been an informant of his going back several years. But he was testifying before the magistrate on the lothHaresh case, leaving Danthres to work this particular murder alone.

"I need you to give me the person whom you sent to sleep with Erot Vospoyt."

Suzett winced. "I am truly sorry, Detective, but I cannot do that."

Danthres gritted her teeth. She knew she should have just waited until tomorrow to let Torin handle this. "I don't have time for games, Suzett. I've already spoken to Vospoyt's family and his servants. They all said that Erot hired someone from your establishment to have sex with him, and they all heard the result of that request, as it echoed throughout the halls despite a Silence Spell." Danthres didn't add that Laula Vospoyt, the matriarch of the family, went on at some length with regards to the words she was going to have with the proprietor of the magick shop from whence she obtained said spell, as it did not do as advertised, and they all heard every "horrid copulation," as she put it. Not to mention what happened at the end.

"I'm not denying that we provided Erot's companionship, Detective."

"Good. Because said companion left Erot's body beaten and bloody and bruised and, finally, dead, after several heroic attempts made by a healer to avert that last bit. Your employee is a murderer, Suzett, and I am very much not interested in your attempts to protect him or her."

At that last part, Suzett's lips turned ever-so-slightly. "I'm afraid, Detective, that neither pronoun is appropriate. Erot was not interested in *human* companionship." She looked away. "And I *did* warn him. In fact, I specifically requested that he sign a waiver."

"A waiver?" This conversation had taken a turn Danthres had not anticipated. She hated performing interrogations where she didn't know what to expect.

It turned out that Suzett wasn't looking away out of embarrassment, but was instead peering through the beads. She then went back into the office, the beads clacking against each other as she displaced them.

Danthres followed her in. Suzett rummaged through assorted scrolls on her small desk until she found one.

As she handed it over to Danthres, Suzett said, "It's very dangerous to try to have sex with a hobgoblin, but Erot is—was—a customer in very good standing, as are many members of the Vospoyt family. That standing is both why I was willing to accede to his rather unique request, and also why I insisted on the waiver. In fact—"

Holding up a gauntleted hand, Danthres said, "Stop!"

"Detective?"

"Can we go back to the first sentence?"

"When I asked what you could do for me?"

"Not that far, the part about how Erot's companion was a damn *hobgoblin*!"

Suzett blinked. "You didn't know?"

"*No*, I didn't know! I'm fairly certain the rest of the family didn't know, either."

"Oh, dear."

Holding up the waiver, Danthres said, "I need to hang onto this."

"Of course. I anticipated that something like this might happen, and I have an additional copy for my own records."

Danthres gritted her teeth again. "Of course. I also still need the hobgoblin."

"And I still cannot provide it for you, Detective. Not," she added quickly before Danthres could retort, "because I do not wish to, but because I no longer have possession of the creature. I rented it from a service. It was ensorcelled with a spell that would compel it to return here when its work was completed, and then the service retook possession of it."

At this rate, Danthres would have no teeth left. "I will need the name and location of the service, please."

As Suzett rummaged in the paperwork on her desk to secure that information for her, Danthres wondered how, exactly, she was going to explain to the Vospoyts that it was a hobgoblin, not a prostitute, who killed their son.

Maybe she'd wait until morning, let Torin do it...

Don't Ask the Question if You Don't Want the Answer

LIEUTENANT MANFRED WAS FINISHING UP PAPERWORK ON THE ROBBERY HE and Lieutenant Kellan had closed when he heard voices entering the squadroom.

"Look, it's not something I'm comfortable with," said a female voice that Manfred identified as belonging to Lieutenant Aleta lothLathna.

"Why not?" That was Manfred's partner Kellan. "C'mon, Aleta, it's a reasonable question."

As they entered the squadroom, Manfred looked up as the pair walked in, along with Aleta's partner, the newly promoted Lieutenant Horran.

"He's right," Horran was saying. "I mean, what if we get some shitbrain who took a Strength Spell or something?"

"What's going on?" Manfred asked.

Kellan looked over at him. "Oh, hey, Manfred, you're still here? I thought you were finishing up the paperwork on the Coosk case?"

He held up a scroll. "Just needs you to sign it, partner."

"Great!" Kellan came over to his desk and grabbed a quill.

As he affixed his signature to the scroll, Kellan said, "We're tryin' to get Aleta to admit to how she would put down a crazy perp."

Manfred grinned. "You mean what fancy Shranlaseth technique she'd use, right?"

Aleta had moved over to her desk and sat down. "I'm sorry, Horran, Kellan, but I'm just not particularly comfortable with sharing these techniques. Besides, it's not as if you could duplicate them."

"Why the hell not?" Horran asked, sounding very offended.

"Because Shranlaseth training takes decades. It's not something I can just show you how to do in a squadroom in five minutes."

Holding up both hands, Horran said, "Look, I don't need you to *teach* me or nothin'. I ain't interested in becoming part of the elf secret police, y'know? I just wanna know *how* you'd do it. I mean, c'mon, we're partners now, I wanna know whatcha can do."

Aleta let out a long breath. "It depends on what you wish to do. Kellan, may I borrow you?"

Kellan shrugged. "Yeah, I guess."

He walked over to her desk as she got back to her feet. "If I just want to incapacitate him, this arm grip —"

"*Ow!*" Kellan cried out as Aleta grabbed his right arm.

Manfred winced as Aleta twisted his partner's right arm behind his back.

" — will do the trick. Now if he's still struggling, you do a kick to his instep —"

She picked up her right foot and kicked straight down onto Kellan's left leg. Kellan screamed in agony as he collapsed onto the floor.

Aleta was still holding one arm, but Kellan was now clutching his left leg with the same-sided arm, and moaning incoherently.

" — and then he'll collapse to the floor." She knelt down, her knees resting on his side. "Kneeling down like this, he can't move, at least in theory. Now if he really does have a Strength Spell, or if he just needs to be put down, then you need to just break his neck, which is usually pretty hard, but if you just grip the neck in the right place —"

"AAAAHHH — kkkkkkkkkk —" Kellan went limp, eyes shut.

" — it works."

Horran looked on in horror. "What did you —?"

Before Manfred could say anything about his newly late partner, Captain Dru came out of his office.

"What the hell's all the —" He looked at Aleta, who was now standing over Kellan's prose form. "Oh, for — Dammit, Aleta, what did I tell you about killing your fellow detectives?"

Horran's jaw was now drooping so far open it was practically on the floor. "What did she — it — he —"

Dru looked over at Horran in concern. "You okay, Horran?"

"What's wrong?" Aleta asked.

"*You just killed Kellan, for Wiate's sake!*"

Shrugging, Dru said, "Yeah, she does that a lot. We lose more lieutenants that way. That's the problem with having ex-Shranlaseth around. On the other hand, makes it easier on the magistrate—she just kills the suspects, saves time."

"I—it—he—"

And then Dru, Manfred, Aleta, and Kellan all burst out laughing.

Horran stared at each of them. "What's—I don't—"

Aleta held out a hand to help Kellan to his feet. "Very well done—the fall was particularly good, much better than last time."

Manfred nodded. "Yeah, last time the fall didn't really convince me."

"What is wrong with you people?!" Horran shouted.

"What," Dru said, "you didn't think we really let Aleta go around murderin' detectives, didja?"

"Besides," Aleta said, "even I can't snap a neck with my fingers. And I haven't killed a suspect yet, despite what *everyone* seems to think." That last was said with a glower at Manfred.

"Hey, I thought it was a reasonable question at the time," Manfred said defensively.

"You pieces of shit," Horran said.

Dru was grinning, however. "Aleta an' I pulled this on Kellan, an' then on Manfred, back when all three of 'em got promoted after Lord Albin died. You were next."

Horran shook his head. "You scared the hell outta me, you shit-brains."

Holding up both hands, Aleta said, "Mission accomplished, then."

"Y'know, I thought this hazing shit was done with after I stopped bein' a rookie."

"Rookie guard, yeah," Dru said, "but you're a rookie detective now. Starts all over again."

"Great." Horran went to his desk, snatched off his earth-colored cloak petulantly, and sat angrily down, dropping his cloak on the floor. Manfred wondered if he was considering abandoning it and going back to day-shift guard patrol in Mermaid Precinct.

Manfred got up from his desk to file the paperwork, chuckling to himself. He'd been just as pissed when Dru, Aleta, and Kellan had pulled it on him, but by the time the shift had ended, he'd been laughing his ass off with the others when they recounted the story at the Old Ball and Chain. He was pretty sure Horran would as well.

And he'd help sell it to the next rookie, too…

Gan Brightblade and the Swamp of Kormak

To look at Gan Brightblade and Bogg, as they stood on the edge of the swamp, you would not imagine them to be friends.

While both were human and male and muscular, the resemblance ended there. Gan was tall and well groomed, dressed in light chainmail. Bogg wore only a loincloth and boots, as well as a back harness for his sword.

"What the hell're we *doin'* here, Gan?" Bogg asked. He slapped his arm, where a mosquito had landed. "Where *is* here, anyhow?"

"This is the Castle Aviva," Gan said.

"This is a damned swamp."

"Yes," Gan said gravely, "the castle has long stood in part due to being surrounded by the fearsome Swamp of Kormak. Once, it was home to mighty warlords and evil wizards."

"'Once'? So not now?"

"Er, no," Gan said.

"So why do I give a shit?" Bogg leaned against one of the many large trees that surrounded the swamp, camouflaging the castle and its natural moat.

"I suppose you should not. But now it is the stronghold of the gang of brigands known as the Roffmin Brigade."

"Those're the shit-suckers who kidnap people, right?"

Gan nodded. "And they have taken Mari, Nari, and Genero."

"How the hell'd *that* happen?" Mari and Nari were halfing twins, and also thieves, while Genero was a priest of Temisa. The five of them, along with the elven sorcerer Olthar lothSirhans and the dwarven general Ubàrlig, had fought against some of the mightiest foes in all Flingaria.

So Bogg found it hard to believe that they were just kidnapped.

"I'm afraid I cannot speak to that. All I'm aware of is that they were taken. Olthar and Ubàrlig are unavailable, so it is left to you and I to rescue them."

"Why'd they kidnap 'em, anyhow?"

"Their usual method is to offer a ransom. In this case, it was made to the bishopric in Velessa. However, the Temisans prefer not to ransom their priests, so it is left to us to rescue them."

"So what're we waitin' for?" Pushing himself off the tree, Bogg started to move toward the swamp.

But Gan held him back. "Hold, my friend. The reason why this castle has been such a stronghold for so long is because of the terrors that lurk beneath the swamp. There are no bridges that traverse it, and the muck itself is filled with perils to chill the soul! There are dragon turtles and piranhas, quippers and chuuls. It will take all of our considerable skill to traverse this swamp—but it shall be worth it! For Genero, Mari, and Nari are our comrades in blood, and they must be rescued! I have been preparing for this encounter since I first heard the news, and while I'd hoped that Olthar and Ubàrlig would join us as well, I'm sure that— Bogg, *what* are you doing?"

While Gan had been going on, Bogg had been looking at the tree he'd been leaning against. Specifically, he was looking up at the trunk, which extended very far into the sky, and which was undecorated by leaves, despite it being a warm summer day. "This thing's dead. And that means it'd be pretty easy for a coupla strong guys like you 'n' me to knock over."

"To what end?"

"You said there wasn't a bridge. Let's you an' me make one."

Gan stared at his friend for several seconds. He'd been steeling himself for the ordeal of facing the aquatic creatures that lurked in the Kormak Swamp for days now. So it took him the better part of a minute to readjust himself to the realization that, if Bogg was right—and while the barbarian from the north was no scholar, he knew the ways of destruction—they could turn this dead tree into a bridge that would take them past all the perils of the swamp.

The two humans stood on the side of the dead tree that faced away from the swamp and pushed with all their might. Sinews formed by the hard life of those in the north and by a lifetime of armed conflict eventually forced the tree's dried-up roots to abandon their purchase in the ground.

The massive tree fell into the swamp with a mighty squelch. Gan and Bogg saw that the top of the tree was brushing against the castle's front door.

Bogg grinned, showing very few teeth. "Let's go get the stupid priest an' the idiot twins outta hock, Gan."

Clapping his barbarian friend on the back, Gan said, "So it shall be, my friend — so it shall be!"

The Streak

"So do we have any idea who this guy is?" Lieutenant Arn Kellan asked.

Jared, the guard assigned to Dragon Precinct who'd discovered the dead body in the house, said, "Besides dead? No. Ain't the owner, though. Lady who called us 'cause'a the smell said he ain't the owner."

Kellan's partner, Lieutenant Manfred, asked, "Does this witness know who the owner is?"

"A dwarf, name'a Granborlanig."

"Has anyone seen Granborlanig lately?"

"She said she last saw 'im this mornin'."

Manfred nodded. "All right, let's talk to her."

Wincing, Jared said, "She ain't gonna be much help. I just toldja everythin' she said, an' it took me the whole half-hour it took you two t'walk here from the castle t'get that much. Better off waitin' for the M.E."

Kellan shook his head. "Boneen's off at some kind of wizard's retreat all week. So no magickal examiner on this case. We're on our own."

"Shit." Jared grinned. "Guess that streak's in jeopardy, huh?"

Now Kellan turned on his partner. "There anyone you *haven't* told about the streak?"

"What, we closed eight cases in a row! Why *shouldn't* I talk about it?"

Rolling his eyes, Kellan said, "Fine, whatever. We've just been lucky."

"Says you. I think it proves that we're brilliant, and should've been promoted years ago."

Kellan started to argue then decided against it.

The two lieutenants left the house, which smelled awful — the whole reason why they were called in the first place — and met with the witness out front.

"You're the next-door neighbor?" Manfred asked.

The woman nodded. "Name's Jannett."

"You called this in?"

"Yah. Place smells like shit. I got kids, they can't be smellin' that every day."

Kellan asked, "You last saw Granborlanig, the owner, this morning?"

"That's right, yeah. Had him a big thick satchel, too, like he was plannin' to go someplace."

"Shit," Kellan muttered.

While that piece of information was more than Jared got, they got very little beyond that. After letting her go back to her home, Kellan looked at Manfred. "I think the streak is dead."

"Why you say that? This Granborlanig shitbrain has to be our guy."

"Of course he is! Body smells that bad, it's been there at least a couple days, but he was here this morning. Pretty sure he would've let someone know if he wasn't the one who did it, and pretty sure he wouldn't have packed a bag and left if he didn't. He's probably on a boat in the middle of the Garamin Sea at this point."

Manfred looked like he wanted to argue, but while his lips kept twitching, he had no actual answer to Kellan's point.

"This is why the streak shit is nonsense, by the way," Kellan said. "I used to think you just had to be smart to close a case, but there's so much other shit involved. I mean, we've *solved* this case, but we can't close it without Granborlanig showing up."

"Excuse me?"

Kellan and Manfred both turned around to see a dwarf carrying a very large satchel.

The dwarf continued: "What are you two guards doing in front of my house?"

Manfred looked at Kellan. Kellan looked at Manfred. They both looked back at the dwarf.

Slowly, Manfred asked, "Um, are you Granborlanig?"

"Yup." Then his eyes widened. "Oh, wait, you're here about the dead body, aren't you?"

"So you know about that."

"Um, yeah. And I'd be more than happy to help you investigate this horrible crime! I mean, can you imagine my surprise at coming home yesterday and finding a dead body in my house?"

Kellan bit back a guffaw with a sudden coughing fit. Manfred kept a straighter face as he said, "I gotta say, I'm having trouble imagining it."

"Well, it's true! I have no idea *who* that man is, or how he wound up dead in my house!"

"And why didn't you contact the Castle Guard yourself?"

"Um, well, you see, I had some errands to run this morning."

Manfred nodded. "And you say you found the body last night?"

"Yeah."

"And left this morning to run errands?"

"Yeah."

"And slept all night in the house with a dead body in it, instead of summoning the Guard?"

"Um." Granborlanig cleared his throat. "Well, it was late. At night, I mean. You guys were probably asleep. I didn't want to bother you. And this morning, like I said, I had errands."

"Uh huh." Manfred looked at Kellan, who was still coughing. "Look, I think you should come with us to the castle. We should talk about what happened there."

"Sure, that'd be fine. I really want to help you guys find out who killed poor Uriik."

Manfred and Kellan exchanged another glance. Kellan started coughing again. Manfred said, "I thought you didn't know who it was."

"Oh, well, you see, um, I—" Granborlanig swallowed. "Lucky guess?"

"You'd better come with us," Manfred said, grabbing the dwarf's arm. Then he looked at Kellan. "The streak is *real*."

Kellan just shook his head.

ABOUT THE AUTHOR

KEITH R.A. DeCANDIDO IS A WHITE MALE IN HIS LATE FORTIES, APPROX-
imately two hundred pounds. He was last seen in the wilds of the
Bronx, New York City, though he is often sighted in other locales.
Usually he is armed with a laptop computer, which some have classified
as a deadly weapon. Through use of this laptop, he has inflicted more
than fifty novels, as well as an indeterminate number of comic books,
nonfiction, novellas, and works of short fiction on an unsuspecting
reading public. Many of these are set in the milieus of television shows,
games, movies, and comic books, among them *Star Trek, Alien, Cars,
Summoners War, Doctor Who, Supernatural, World of Warcraft*, Marvel
Comics, and many more.

We have received information confirming that more stories involving Danthres, Torin, and the city-state of Cliff's End can be found in the
novels *Dragon Precinct, Unicorn Precinct, Goblin Precinct, Gryphon
Precinct*, and the forthcoming *Phoenix Precinct* and *Manticore Precinct*, as
well as the short-story collections *Tales from Dragon Precinct* and the
forthcoming *More Tales from Dragon Precinct*. His other recent crimes
against humanity include *A Furnace Sealed*, the debut of a new urban
fantasy series taking place in DeCandido's native Bronx; the *Alien* novel
Isolation; the *Marvel's Tales of Asgard* trilogy of prose novels starring Marvel's versions of Thor, Sif, and the Warriors Three; short stories in the
anthologies *Aliens: Bug Hunt, Joe Ledger: Unstoppable, The Best of Bad-Ass
Faeries, The Best of Defending the Future, TV Gods: Summer Programming,
X-Files: Trust No One, Nights of the Living Dead*, the award-winning
Planned Parenthood benefit anthology *Mine!*, the two *Baker Street Irreg-
ulars* anthologies, and *Release the Virgins!*; and articles about pop culture
for Tor.com and on his own Patreon.

If you see DeCandido, do not approach him, but call for backup immediately. He is often seen in the company of a suspicious-looking woman who goes by the street name of "Wrenn," as well as several as-yet-unidentified cats. A full dossier can be found at DeCandido.net

CPSIA information can be obtained
at www.ICGtesting.com
Printed in the USA
LVHW041711180619
621610LV00002B/221